Michael was too much to deny herself any longer.

Even as she worried that she might be nothing more than his prey, she was more than willing. She wanted this with everything she had.

He dipped his head lower and his lips brushed her neck, his stubble scratching her. His hair fell forward as he kissed her neck, his mouth now open, his warm tongue making her lose her mind. It felt so good she wanted to close her eyes and languish in every heavenly sensation. For that moment, she seemed like she might be everything to him, precisely what she had once hoped to be.

He hooked his thumbs into her dress straps and pulled them down her shoulders. He gathered her hair in one hand and kissed his way across her back, sending waves of tingles along her spine. His lips weren't just warm, they were on fire. His kiss was urgent. He pressed his long body against hers; his knees met the back of her thighs and his chest met her shoulders. She pushed right back into him, their bodies grinding against each other as she rolled her head to the other side.

"I want you," she murmured, almost involuntarily.

A rough groan left the depths of his throat. "That's a very good thing, Charlie. I'm not sure I could live through it if you didn't."

* * *

Little Secrets: Holiday Baby Bombshell
is part of the Little Secrets series—Untamed
passion, unexpected pregnancy...

Dear Reader,

Thank you for picking up *Little Secrets: Holiday Baby Bombshell*! It's not only part of Little Secrets, it's the second book in the Locke Legacy series, about the Locke family of New York, set against the backdrop of their historic Manhattan hotel, The Grand Legacy.

The star of this story is Charlotte, the youngest Locke sibling, the one member of the family who can't quite get her act together. She's had every career under the sun and still hasn't found her groove. So when she decides to ask her brother for the real estate listings on the new condos in The Grand Legacy, it's more than a bump in the road when she discovers that he'll only give her half. The other half is going to her ex-boyfriend, Michael Kelly. Michael is a former competitive swimmer who doesn't know where competition stops and real life begins.

He and Charlotte are racing to see who can sell out first, which lent itself to some of my favorite scenes in the book. These two can hurtle some fun and furious banter. Charlotte's not only determined to prove to her family that she can be capable, but she's dead set on handing Michael, aka Mr. Perfect, a crushing defeat. She wants him to know what it's like to lose... even if it's only a onetime thing. Of course, when he learns her secret, he must face the prospect of losing even more.

I hope you enjoy this second-chance rivalry story! Drop me a line anytime at karen@karenbooth.net. I love hearing from readers!

Karen

KAREN BOOTH

—

LITTLE SECRETS: HOLIDAY BABY BOMBSHELL

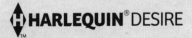

HARLEQUIN® DESIRE

Recycling programs
for this product may
not exist in your area.

ISBN-13: 978-0-373-83880-6

Little Secrets: Holiday Baby Bombshell

Copyright © 2017 by Karen Booth

This edition published by arrangement with Harlequin Books S.A.

For questions and comments about the quality of this book, please contact us at CustomerService@Harlequin.com.

Printed in U.S.A.

www.Harlequin.com

Karen Booth is a Midwestern girl transplanted in the South, raised on '80s music, Judy Blume and the films of John Hughes. She writes sexy big-city love stories. When she takes a break from the art of romance, she's teaching her kids about good music, honing her Southern cooking skills or sweet-talking her husband into whipping up a batch of cocktails. Find out more about Karen at karenbooth.net.

Books by Karen Booth

Harlequin Desire

That Night with the CEO
Pregnant by the Rival CEO
The CEO Daddy Next Door
The Best Man's Baby
The Ten-Day Baby Takeover

The Locke Legacy

Pregnant by the Billionaire

Little Secrets

Little Secrets: Holiday Baby Bombshell

Visit her Author Profile page at Harlequin.com, or karenbooth.net, for more titles.

For my sweet and endlessly patient husband.
I'm writing as fast as I can in the hopes
that you can retire early.

One

With its French-milled soap, lavender-scented shampoo and soft lighting, the finely appointed bathroom in her Grand Legacy Hotel suite might've been the loveliest place Charlotte Locke had ever gotten sick. She closed her eyes, willed herself to stand from the cool comfort of the marble floor and fumbled for her toothbrush. Ten weeks pregnant and mint was one of the few things she found appealing. She scrubbed her teeth clean, straightened her skirt and jacket, and neatened her blond hair. Hopefully, that was the last of today's morning sickness. She had work to do.

Charlotte marched out of her room, determined. "Wish me luck. I'm off to Sawyer's office," she said to her aunt Fran, who was sharing the suite while in New York from London for Christmas.

Fran tucked a strand from her white-blond bob behind her ear, then refilled her mug with room-service tea. Charlotte's beloved papillon dog, Thor, nine pounds of snow-white and chocolate-brown attitude, was curled up at Fran's hip. "You won't need luck. You're more than qualified to sell the Grand Legacy condos."

Charlotte sighed. Okay, no luck. But she wouldn't mind some bolstering. How many times had she gone hat-in-hand and asked a family member for another chance? Too many. Charlotte slipped on her wool coat, a lovely shade of peacock blue, and buttoned up. "I'm glad you're so confident. I think I stand about a fifty-fifty chance."

"You're sure you aren't going to tell Sawyer about the pregnancy? He's your brother. I don't see any way he can say no to you if he knows you have a baby on the way."

Charlotte shook her head. "I don't want anyone's charity. I'm asking him to trust me with millions of dollars of real estate. I don't want to remind him that his little sister has a habit of making colossal life mistakes."

Fran scratched Thor behind the ear. "Everything happens for a reason. It just might not be clear to you yet what that reason is."

"I like your optimism, but being accidentally pregnant by a man who doesn't love me is classic Charlotte. I'm trying to avoid all appearances of the old me." Charlotte leaned down and kissed her aunt's cheek, then grabbed her gloves and handbag and stepped out into the hall, closing the door behind her.

Each impeccable detail of the Grand Legacy—the plush black carpet with ornate royal blue scrolls, the gleaming chrome-and-glass wall sconces, even the tasteful sign directing guests to their room—was a link to Charlotte's past. The hotel had been in her family since the 1920s, long before she'd been born. Now it was solely owned by her brother Sawyer, a detail that displeased their father greatly.

She pushed the button for the elevator. Every time she stepped on board, childhood memories of clowning around in the hotel with her brothers played in her head, like an old movie. The ones where she was youngest were the fuzziest, but the happiest. There had been many games of hide-and-seek in these halls, but only when her mother had been alive. As soon as she passed away, their father never wanted her or her brothers to spend any time at all in the hotel.

"Good morning, Ms. Locke," a bellman said as she emerged from the elevator.

"Morning," she said cheerily. Her heels clicked across the black-and-white marble lobby floor.

"Stay warm out there, Ms. Locke," the front desk clerk said.

"I'll try." She pushed her way through the revolving doors and was smacked in the face with a rush of icy air that felt as though it had been shipped in from the north pole. The doorman hustled to show her to the car Sawyer had sent.

"Thank you." Charlotte juggled her wallet, a five-dollar bill and her gloves.

"That's not necessary, Ms. Locke." He tried to hand back the tip. "Not from you."

"Of course it's necessary. You work hard, and it's the holidays." She smiled, waved him off and slid into the back seat of the car.

The driver knew exactly where they were headed—downtown to Sawyer's office in Chelsea. Charlotte had already practiced her pitch several times—awake in bed last night, in the shower that morning. It wasn't that Sawyer was intimidating. He was anything but. It was more that Charlotte hated to ask for yet another favor. She was already bracing for that look on her brother's face, the one that said he was hesitant to give her responsibility. She'd done so poorly with it in the past.

Charlotte couldn't commit any more time or effort to feeling bad about her current situation. Now was the time for action. The car pulled up in front of Sawyer's office, and she wasted no time climbing out and heading upstairs. Hopefully inertia would be enough to keep her going.

Her brother's admin, Lily, greeted her warmly. "Your brother is waiting. Let me take your coat for you. Remind me when you get out of your meeting and I'll call another car for you."

"Thank you so much." Charlotte smoothed her skirt, trying to ignore the trepidation in her stomach. This was her brother. Sawyer. Everything would be fine. She hoped.

A broad smile crossed Sawyer's face when she poked her head into his office. "There she is."

Waves of relief washed over her. Why she constantly worked herself into a tizzy over things was beyond her. She only knew it was her habit. "Hey, Sawyer. Thanks for meeting with me today."

"Of course. I'm glad you came in. I feel like I hardly had the chance to speak to you at the grand reopening party at the hotel."

"Sorry about that. All sorts of old friends were there." *Plus, pregnancy makes a woman all kinds of tired.*

"I'm just glad you're back in town. It wouldn't have felt right not to have you there." Sawyer sat back in his chair. "Do you want to tell me what precipitated the surprise junket to see Aunt Fran in England?"

Even though she'd prepared for the question, Charlotte blanched at it. So much had led to that trip. It started with the breakup from Michael Kelly, the man she'd fallen hopelessly in love with, the man who was unable to return the feelings. That had been bad enough, and then came the real powder keg—the pregnancy. She couldn't tell her brother she'd gone to

England for those reasons. Charlotte was always falling in love, and it was always getting her into some sort of impossible situation.

"I just needed some time to really think out my long-term career goals. Fran is so good at listening and helping with advice." She cleared her throat. "Plus, I'll be honest. It was stressful to watch the way Dad was fighting you on the Grand Legacy renovation. I hate the family rifts."

"If I could've gone to England with you, I would have. Then again, that might have meant things wouldn't have worked out with Kendall the way they have. So scratch that. I'm glad I stayed and fought through the Dad situation."

Charlotte smiled. She was happy Sawyer had found someone, and Kendall was a very special someone. Charlotte had worried for many years that their home life had left her and her siblings—Sawyer and their brother Noah—incapable of having normal romantic relationships. The fact that Sawyer had finally broken through that particular Locke family glass ceiling gave her hope that some day she'd do the same. Just not anytime soon—she was no longer looking for love. Stability was her number one quest. "I'm really happy for you and Kendall. I'm so looking forward to the wedding. I love the idea of a wedding at Christmastime."

"I know it's soon, but we didn't want to wait. Call

us old-fashioned, but we both want to tie the knot before the baby arrives."

"Sure. Wouldn't want your little boy or girl to do the math later in life and figure out you were married after the fact." Charlotte couldn't believe what was coming out of her own mouth. She sounded like her grandmother. Maybe she was just as old-fashioned as her brother. She'd be putting an end to that soon, though, with her very single status while welcoming a new life into the world.

"So, tell me about these long-term career goals. You aren't considering a change from real estate, are you?"

This was a valid question where Charlotte was concerned. The number of careers she'd had in her twenties was enough to make anyone's head spin— interior designer, fashion blogger, party planner, cupcake maven. That last one had been the most disastrous. Charlotte couldn't cook to save her life and she'd gained fifteen pounds tasting buttercream all day long.

"Nope. It's still the right career for me. It's a natural fit with the real-estate development and hotel interests in our family. It allows me to work with people, which I love doing. And the good side of having had so many false starts with various careers is that I've made a ton of contacts." *Watch me make lemonade with my arms full of lemons.*

"I'm glad to hear you've settled on it. That stability will be good for you."

"Exactly. Stability." Charlotte sucked in a deep breath. *Here goes nothing.* "And that's why I'm here. Now that you've put the finishing touches on the Grand Legacy condos, I'm hoping you'll let me have the listings." Charlotte couldn't help but notice how her brother's expression had fallen. She had to make her case now, or lose out. "I know the building better than any agent you could possibly work with. You know that it will have my full attention, and more than anything, it will give us a chance to work closely together, which is something I've always wanted to do."

"But, Charlotte…you can't just pop in here and ask for the listings now. I've been working on this for months. This is so like you to throw a wrench in things at the eleventh hour."

Yeah, well, I didn't exactly plan on getting pregnant. "I know. I'm sorry about the timing, but nobody expected the units to be ready now. Your original opening date was New Year's Eve. That's still several weeks away."

Sawyer pressed his lips together firmly, seeming deep in thought. "I already have an agent lined up. A fantastic one who will most likely sell every unit in a matter of weeks. He's on his way over right now to discuss strategy and to get the paperwork straightened away."

"But…" Charlotte had already discharged her only arguments. She didn't really have any other means of selling herself. She was, as always, an unproven proposition. "I'm family. Surely that counts for something. It's the Grand Legacy. This isn't some random building you and Noah decided to sink money into." She could see Sawyer's eyes soften and she knew she had to open up her heart. "I love the hotel so much, and being there over the last few days has been amazing. Isn't it important to have someone who really, truly cares?"

"You don't know that this other agent doesn't care. I've had multiple conversations with Michael Kelly about this over the last few months and I can tell you that he absolutely cares."

Charlotte's heart had stopped beating. Or at least it felt that way. Unwanted visions of Michael popped into her head—all six feet and six inches of his trim and muscled swimmer's body. He might have crushed her heart, but he'd looked good doing it, with his thick, dark hair she loved to comb her fingers through, and magnetic blue eyes she could get lost in for days. "Michael Kelly? Seriously?"

"Do you know him? He's a really good guy. Straight shooter. He cares a lot. He's told me so."

Charlotte blew out a breath. Michael Kelly cared, all right—about himself, money and his job. Everyone else was going to have to fend for themselves.

* * *

Michael knew he didn't have much more time in the pool this morning. *Just a few more laps.* He touched the tile wall with his hand and took his turn, propelling himself through the water, beneath the surface, to return to the other end.

The rhythm of swimming relaxed him. After tens of thousands of hours spent in the pool, his muscles knew exactly what to do, and he could give his brain some space to roam. This was the only time during his day that he was unreachable, his cell phone turned off and tucked away in his personal locker at the brand-new Empire State Athletic Club, an expensive and exclusive replacement for the old Downtown Athletic Club, which had been converted to apartments years ago. He loved this sliver of his day, when he had a chance to unplug. Owning and running the top residential real-estate agency in the city, The Kelly Group, meant that he was otherwise expected to be available 24/7, 365 days a year.

He made another turn and switched to freestyle, the stroke that had won him three Olympic golds. He always ended his swim this way. It was a powerful reminder of what had once been, of everything he'd worked so hard for and, most important, what it felt like to win. Coming out on top was a high unlike any other, and after his retirement from swimming six years ago, he'd been working his butt off in real estate just to get a taste of that feeling. He lived for that moment when you're invincible, standing at the top of the mountain, looking down at everyone else that couldn't match up to you. There was no roar of the crowd or medals awarded in real estate, but the money helped. And there had been a lot of it, not that there wasn't always more to earn.

He skimmed along in the water at the end of his final lap, came to the surface, pulled off his swim cap and tossed it onto the pool deck. He scooped water into his hair and hoisted himself up out of the pool, grabbing his towel. There was one other person still in the pool—Gabe Underwood. Gabe had taken up swimming a year ago, when he also set his sights on knocking Michael from his perch of top-selling real-estate agent in Manhattan. Gabe certainly knew he wasn't in the same league as Michael when it came to the sport that had won him Olympic medals, but he insisted that he wanted to remind Michael that he was on his heels and closing in.

It was annoying, but Michael couldn't stop the guy from swimming laps at the same time he did. They were both members of the club, and all the money in the world wasn't going to help Michael put an Olympic swimming pool in a Manhattan apartment. That would have to be for later in life, when he retired out in the Hamptons or Connecticut.

Michael trailed into the locker room and quickly took a shower. The hot water felt fantastic on his muscles. There was definitely a part of him that could have stood beneath the spray for a long period of time, but he had to be on his way. Sawyer Locke and the Grand Legacy apartments were waiting. Towel wrapped around his waist, Michael made his way into the dressing area, where his suit was waiting, freshly pressed by the club staff. His black leather Italian wingtips had been given a polish as well.

"I beat my own time today, Kelly. I'm making big progress." Gabe's voice grated on Michael like little else.

"Yeah? Good for you." *Like I care.* He went ahead with getting dressed, hoping Gabe would take a hint, hit the showers and leave him the hell alone.

"Just like I'm closing in on you in sales. With everything I have lined up for January and February, I'm very close to replacing you as the top agent in the city next year. I have to say, it'll be a sweet reward and very well-earned."

Michael didn't want to take the bait. He wasn't going to take it, but damn, it was hard. Michael fed on competition, but he couldn't let someone see that he cared about their achievements. Focusing on his own was the best way to maintain the steely demeanor necessary for winning. "I'll keep doing what I do, but thanks for the heads-up."

Completely uninvited, Gabe perched on the locker-room bench. "What do you have in the hopper these days? Anything new and exciting? Some big fish on the line?"

"Always. But I'm not about to share that information with you."

"I heard you landed the Grand Legacy residential units."

Dammit. Michael worked his feet into his shoes. He wasn't about to spill the details. It was all sewn up, but there was no point in bragging. He'd let news of the sales filter through the circles of the real-estate world on their own.

"No comment?" Gabe asked. "I get it. Trying to be the mysterious Michael Kelly. Well, I'm psyched for you, but just so you know, I've worked on several properties with Sawyer's brother, Noah. I even snagged an invitation to Sawyer's wedding. Pretty sure those guys are eager to work with me."

Michael cast his eyes at Gabe, but only for a moment. The less he acknowledged him, the better. "I know the game you're playing because I invented it. Don't try to go up against me. You'll only regret it."

"Is that some sort of threat?"

"I don't need to make threats, Gabe. Threats are for people who can't deliver. I always deliver." With that, Michael grabbed his suit coat. "Have a good day."

Michael strode to the elevator and took it down to the parking garage, where his car was waiting. He was one of those guys—the ones who insisted on having a car in the city, even when it was generally a pain in the butt. He didn't like waiting around for other people, he didn't like barking orders from the back seat. He knew the best way to get where he wanted to go, and driving himself was the only way to get there.

Traffic wasn't too heavy, so he arrived at Sawyer Locke's office in twenty minutes and nabbed a spot in the lot next to his building. He took the stairs and still arrived five minutes early.

"Please have a seat, Mr. Kelly. Mr. Locke is finishing up a conversation with his sister. Can I get you a cup of coffee while you wait?"

His sister? Charlotte's back in town? Michael shifted in his seat, finding it more than a bit uncomfortable. "Uh, No, thank you. I've had two cups already this morning."

"It shouldn't be more than a few minutes."

Michael had learned long ago that there's a bump in every road, especially when you're sure everything is going to go smoothly. Apparently, today's bump was going to be Charlotte. He'd probably jinxed himself by daring to think the Grand Legacy was a done deal. Now he had to hope that Sawyer didn't mention who his ten o'clock was with, opening the door for Charlotte to rail on Michael, call him a jerk or insensitive or any of the things she'd called him the day she'd ended it with him.

The thing was, Michael had had no choice but to open the door for Charlotte to break things off with him. Three months of monogamy was a lifetime for him, and all signs were there that Charlotte was taking things much more seriously than he ever would be able to. He just wasn't built for focusing on a relationship. There was nothing to win. He'd be lying if he said he was looking forward to speaking to Charlotte. He could only imagine what she might spout off at him. But he was most certainly looking forward to *seeing* her, even if it might be as she huffed and stormed past him in the lobby of her brother's office.

Lily's phone buzzed. "Yes, Mr. Locke?" She glanced over at Michael. "Certainly. I'll send him right in." She hung up and rose from her seat. "Mr. Locke will see you now." She stepped out from behind her desk and headed for Sawyer's office.

"I thought you said he was meeting with Charlotte."

Surprise crossed Lily's face. "You know Ms. Locke?" She gently tapped her forehead. "Of course you know Ms. Locke. You both work in real estate."

Michael cleared his throat. *That's not the only reason.* "We're acquainted."

"Well, good. Mr. Locke won't need to make any introductions."

Michael was beyond confused, eyeing the door as Lily rapped on it lightly. "I'm sorry. I guess I'm running a step slow today. My meeting was with Sawyer. It's an important one, too. If he's busy, perhaps I should come back another time." *And cut out of here before Charlotte lops off my head.*

The door opened. Sawyer waved him in. "Michael. I understand you've already met my sister, Charlotte."

Two

Michael did not like to go into meetings unprepared, but he did love a challenge. He first saw Charlotte only in profile, her long, golden-blond hair framing her rosy cheeks, full lips and adorable chin. She sat straight as a pin in a dark purple jacket and black skirt, poised on the edge of her seat. That was Charlotte. Beautiful, but always on the edge. She turned toward him, her vivid blue eyes immediately putting him on notice. She was still angry. He not only saw it, he felt it, as if her eyes were slicing right into him.

It was pretty hot.

Just seeing her brought back the day they first met seven or eight months ago, when she'd come to interview for a position in his agency. She'd been professional and polished, but her résumé was thin. As they talked, he became more and more enchanted by her as a woman, but he knew she wasn't cutthroat enough to work for him. She smiled so easily, almost as if she couldn't help it. She laughed in much the same, affable manner. She was clearly beguiling, but he couldn't see her playing hardball in a negotiation, or putting up with an ultrademanding billionaire client. He'd told her as much. That hadn't gone over well. In fact, she'd argued with him about it, giving him that first vision of the fire behind those eyes. In the end, she didn't get the job she wanted, but he called her a few weeks later anyway. He asked her out and she said no, but then she started peppering him with questions about real estate, and the next thing he knew, they'd been on the phone for an hour, the conversation ultimately drifting to more personal topics. Three or four more marathon calls after that, he asked her out again, and that time she said yes. The rest—all three months of it—was history.

"Michael, hello." Charlotte's words were polite enough, but the tenor of her voice was rigid. She'd never taken that tone with him before, not even when she left. That day, she'd only had tears and gasping breaths. Crying was one of his weak spots when it came to relationships. He never knew what to say. So he often didn't say much of anything.

"Charlotte. It's nice to see you." He reached out

to shake her hand and it was clear she was thinking twice about it. When she finally reciprocated, she was quick to retreat, but even a lightning-fast brush of her skin against his brought back memories of just how white-hot their connection had been. Charlotte might be a handful, but that was also the reason she was impossible to forget.

She folded her hands in her lap as Michael took the open chair next to her and Sawyer sat behind his desk. Michael's full attention needed to be on Sawyer at this moment, but he had to steal a glance at Charlotte's legs as she crossed them and sat even straighter. She was wearing jet-black heels today, and he would've been a fool not to take his chance to admire her, while his mind flashed to what the rest of her looked like naked as she did the simplest of things, like padding from his bed to the bathroom and back.

"Michael, the reason I've asked Charlotte to sit in on this meeting is because I've decided to make a change with the Grand Legacy condos. I'm giving half of the listings to Charlotte."

Michael always did everything he could to keep his cool in a business meeting, but he did not like surprises. Not at the last minute. "You're what?" His voice betrayed him. The anger was apparent and quite possibly too strong, but as far as he was concerned, he had every right to be mad. He glanced over at Charlotte, only to see her fighting back a smile. He knew that look—the corners of her plump lips twitching while she was trying everything she could not to laugh.

Sawyer held up his hands in defense. "I know this is a surprise, and it's not the way I like to do business, but the timing just wasn't right on this one. You were already on your way here when Charlotte and I talked about it this morning."

"You do realize I can sell those units ten times faster than she can, right?"

Charlotte's hair whipped through the air when she turned to Michael. "Excuse me?" She was no longer close to smiling. Her mouth was slack and gaping with disbelief.

"It's the truth." Michael shrugged and sat back in his chair, reminding himself to stay cool and calm, however angry he might be.

"Look, I hear what you're saying," Sawyer said. "You're a rock star of an agent. There's no denying that."

Tell me something I don't know.

"But Charlotte is family," Sawyer continued. "And she brings some unique qualities to the table that, quite honestly, I hadn't considered and no one else has."

"Like what, exactly?" Michael couldn't imagine that anyone had a talent that he didn't possess. If he was lacking in some way, it had yet to materialize in his life in a formidable way. If he didn't know how to do something, he learned. Quickly.

Charlotte huffed and shook her head. "I have a history with the hotel. I know it almost as well as Sawyer. And I have the Locke name. That counts for something."

She had him on that. "I can always introduce a client to your brother, Charlotte, if they want to meet a member of the Locke family. Of course, at that point, the only name they'll truly care about is mine. They'll get experience with me. How many properties have you even sold since you became an agent?"

"I didn't come here to share my résumé with you. Sawyer doesn't care about that."

"It's not that I don't care about it. I'm simply willing to see past it in order to make a compromise," Sawyer said.

So that's what this was. *A compromise.* Michael was not a fan. "Sawyer, I have buyers lined up. It's just a matter of giving me the go-ahead, and I can start showing units later today."

"I already have a buyer for one unit in the building and she's ready to make a full price offer today," Charlotte piped up.

Michael had plenty of potential buyers and other interested agents on the line already, but no one had seen the condos yet. Sawyer had kept everything under lock and key. "She's bluffing."

Charlotte turned, narrowing her vision on Michael. Her jaw tensed. He could only imagine what was going through that gorgeous head of hers. Murderous thoughts, probably. "I'm not bluffing. I don't need to bluff."

"Then where is this mysterious buyer?"

"You're looking at her." She thrust her chin into the air.

Michael laughed and shook his head at the irony. "You sure you want to do that? You might not like your first neighbor."

"What are you talking about?"

"Michael gave me a verbal offer on a unit for himself a few weeks ago," Sawyer said.

"I'm dying to get into the hotel. It's so much closer to my office. My commute takes way too much time."

"Are you serious?" Charlotte asked.

"The more important question is, are you serious?" Sawyer asked. "It's a big commitment."

Charlotte twisted her lips tightly. "Yes, I'm serious. I need a place to live. I gave up my apartment when I went to England. I'm already living and working out of the hotel. I can quite literally do a showing at any time, day or night. And these apartments will be the only thing I'm working on. You'll have my undivided attention, unlike with another agent, who might be such a hotshot that he's juggling hundreds of properties."

"She might have you there," Sawyer said. "You

can't deny that's a compelling argument for her half of the listings."

Michael had a long string of counterarguments cued up in his head, but the reality was that Charlotte was Sawyer's sister. In Michael's experience, family won out over nearly everything. Sometimes, it even won out over money. Michael needed to focus on his long game, especially with Gabe Underwood on his heels. Sawyer Locke and his brother, Noah, were quickly becoming some of the most prominent real-estate developers in the city. The sooner Michael aligned himself with them, and elbowed Gabe out of the picture, the better. That meant playing ball.

"I'd never want to get in the way of family," Michael said. "I understand it's important you give your sister this opportunity."

"Thank you," Sawyer replied earnestly. "I really appreciate it. Truly. I owe you one."

Music to Michael's ears. "Happy to do it."

"We can get the paperwork in line later today and be on our way." Sawyer rose from his seat. "I'm ready to get these sold. It's one of the final pieces of the puzzle for the Grand Legacy."

"I'm so excited to work together. Thank you so much for the chance," Charlotte said, embracing her brother. That was the reason Michael hadn't stood a chance when he walked into this room. Family bonds were always the strongest.

Sawyer walked them into the lobby, but didn't

have time for long goodbyes, as his admin let him know he had a call. Charlotte was putting on her coat. Purely out of habit, Michael lifted the empty sleeve for her. She yanked it from his hand. "No, thank you. I'm good."

"I'll go down with you."

"I'm taking the stairs."

"Me, too."

"Suit yourself." Charlotte held on to both railings as she descended the stairs, preventing Michael from walking next to her.

He stopped her when they reached the lobby. "Charlotte, hold up for a second." He grasped her arm, but dropped his grip immediately when he saw the disdain on her face. "You gave up your apartment when you went to England? Were you planning on staying?" The timing still seemed odd to him. She'd dumped him, disappeared from his life altogether, and then he'd heard from a friend that she'd run off to Europe without saying goodbye to anyone.

"I didn't know how long I was going to be in London, but my lease was up, so I just put my stuff in storage and left."

Michael shrugged. "Must be nice. Running off at the drop of a hat, no responsibilities to tie you down."

"I was regrouping. And spending time with my aunt."

Regrouping. Michael wasn't sure what that meant, but he knew very well that it was Charlotte's inclination to leave when she had a problem. "You know, you can't run away every time you hit a rough patch. My dad practically drilled that into my head."

"You can stop right there, okay? You don't even know why I went to England. Don't assume."

"So tell me."

"Um, let me think." She set her finger against her temple. "No."

Good God, she was stubborn. "All I'm saying is that you have to keep going when things get tough. This was a problem when we were together. You were always letting the little things get to you. And you were always coming to me with your problems, expecting me to fix everything."

Charlotte nearly blew steam out of her nostrils. "First off, I don't remember asking for your sage life advice. And second, you have a lot to learn about women. I never wanted you to solve my problems. I wanted you to *listen*."

The biting tone she'd taken gave him pause. But only for a second. "Fine, then. I'm listening. Tell me why you went to England."

She glared at him. "It's a little late for listening. Goodbye, Michael." She opened the building door with a shove.

Charlotte. Always the drama queen.

"Dammit," she muttered. "I forgot to have Lily call me a car."

Michael followed her as she shuffled to the curb. "Do you want me to do it? Or I'll call Lily."

She rifled through her handbag, hunched over it while resting it on her leg. "No. I'm fine taking a taxi."

"Then let me give you a ride. I have my car. It's cold out here. You'll freeze."

He took a step toward her and she shot him another one of her piercing looks. Her breaths left her lips in puffs of white and her cheeks began to turn bright pink. "I like the cold."

"No, you don't. You hate it."

"You think you know me, Michael. But you don't. You never took the time."

Clearly, they were having two separate conversations. He didn't have the patience for more of her thinly veiled innuendos about his personal shortcomings. "Okay, then. Have a nice day." He turned and headed for the parking garage.

"I hope you have the worst day ever!" she called back.

Fine. Be like that.

He trudged around the corner and retrieved his car. When he pulled out of the lot, Charlotte was still standing on the sidewalk, looking for a cab. A heavy sigh left his throat. It would be easiest to turn on his blinker, take a right turn and leave Charlotte to fend for herself. But there was this little voice inside him, a voice he normally ignored, suggesting that he might have a few things to make up for, even if he might never know his actual past transgressions because Charlotte spoke in secret code most of the time.

He rolled down his window and the icy air rushed inside. "Charlotte. Come on. I'll give you a ride."

"A cab will come along any minute now," she replied, not looking at him.

The street was dead. *You'd have more luck if you walked over to Seventh Avenue.* "I'll turn on your heated seat."

She glanced back over her shoulder. That flash of her blue eyes was still pretty damn potent from this distance. "Fine."

Shoulders bunched up around her ears, she hurried around to the passenger side as Michael rolled up his window. The instant she climbed inside and closed the door, her sweet vanilla scent hit his nose. Her presence was impossible to ignore in the confines of the car. It sent a powerful wave of recognition through his body. Even with her prickly attitude toward him, if she said she wanted him, he'd go so far as to blow off work for an hour. He never did that for anyone.

"You have to promise you'll drive carefully." She rubbed her hands together in front of the vents. Without asking permission, she reached over and cranked up the heat.

"Charlotte, you know me. There is no such thing as careful."

* * *

Charlotte's heart was beating so fiercely, it didn't even faze her when Michael laid on the horn and yelled at the car in front of him. Everything was getting to her right now, like having the air sucked out of her triumphant announcement that she was going to buy an apartment, only to learn from Michael that he'd made an offer to Sawyer weeks ago. It was bad enough that he'd never said a thing while they were together about cooking up a deal with her brother to sell the Grand Legacy units. It was the perfect illustration of the divide between Michael and Charlotte. A normal couple, a *real* couple, would have discussed such things.

She felt like such a fool, but she had to go through with buying the unit. Her brother knew Charlotte as the woman who made bold, sweeping promises and later changed her mind. Plus, she couldn't stand the thought of Michael being one sale ahead of her.

"Dude. You're killing me with this." Michael jammed the heel of his hand into the car horn again. "Just go."

"See? This is why I didn't want a ride from you. It's more relaxing having a complete stranger take me somewhere."

Michael zipped into the next lane without using a blinker or even looking. "You're in excellent hands."

She slumped back in her seat, unable to ignore the conflicted feelings pinging back and forth between her head and her heart. She hated Michael. Or at least she was trying very hard to. Every logical brain cell in her head knew the reason why—she'd tried harder with him than she had with any other guy, and she still wasn't enough. So why was there some fragment of her that was happy to be in the car with him, even when she also despised his driving? Who had decided that this irrational part of her brain, hopelessly turned on by the vision of his hand wrapped around the gearshift, should have a voice?

She'd spent an awful lot of time during those five weeks in England talking with Aunt Fran about Michael, about the differences between men and women, heartache and the ways in which Charlotte was regularly sabotaging herself. It was good to be open and optimistic, Fran had said, but it wasn't so smart to dive in headfirst every single time. Well, she hadn't quite put it that way. Her exact wording was, *Charlotte, stop picking out your children's names on the first date.* Call it what you will—jumping the gun. Running away with the circus. Going overboard. It was Charlotte's greatest inclination. She knew this about herself.

By all reports, she'd been that way since she was a little girl. Her brothers teased her mercilessly about her endless string of crushes, all of which she'd been stupid enough to identify by name, starting at the age of four with the first boy she ever kissed, Darren Willingham, on the playground in preschool. As the story went, Charlotte had announced her engagement to be married to the unwitting Darren at the dinner table that night. She had no way of knowing if Sawyer and Noah were making up the part of the story where Charlotte produced crayon drawings of her wedding dress, the flowers and the church. The only other witness to the conversation had been their mother, and she'd passed away before Charlotte could ever ask her about it.

Despite the regular razzing from Sawyer and Noah, Charlotte remained undeterred on her quest for love. By the time she was sixteen, she'd figured out that the affection she wasn't getting at home was easily obtained by sneaking out of the house, taking the train into the city and partying all night. It wasn't love, but it was an acceptable substitute, and after a few drinks obtained with a fake ID, a handsome guy flirting with her on the dance floor, wanting to kiss her and hold her and take her home, it sure started to feel like something real. Love had always been Charlotte's drug of choice. She'd wanted it more from Michael than she'd wanted it from any other man.

What a shame she'd invested so much time and effort into the Michael project. She'd killed herself trying to be the perfect girlfriend, making him meals that took hours to prepare because everyone knew what a horrible cook she was. She'd tried to get him to open up about work problems—she could see how stressed he was—but he wasn't big on talking about any of it. Charlotte had been so sure that whatever was wrong, she could make it better. None of her efforts seemed to make much of an impression on him. Maybe it was because he was used to women fawning all over him. Even if that was the case, it still hurt. Of course, cooking and listening had become the least of her worries when she'd finally decided that the best approach with him was a direct one.

She'd planned a romantic evening at his place, bought a gorgeous silk nightgown and had his favorite meal brought in. They'd had dinner that night, they'd made love and Charlotte had waited for the perfect moment to confess her love to Michael. They were curled up in his bed, warm under the covers, lips inches apart. She was just about to profess her love for him when she was preempted by Michael's own confession. He was getting the impression that she wanted a lot more out of their relationship than he was equipped to give. He was too busy for a real girlfriend. It never worked out. *Of course.* It never worked out for Charlotte, either, just for different reasons.

"So? What's your plan?" Michael asked.

If only he knew the true breadth of that question. Her hand instinctively rested on her lower belly. She had a lot to plan for, and a lot to accomplish. It all scared the crap out of her, especially the notion of telling Michael. If he'd managed to anticipate and fend off "I love you," there was zero chance he was up for the challenge of a child. Even so, the baby seemed like the one truly bright spot on her horizon. Motherhood was going to be a lot of work, and she was in no way confident she was up to the task, but she liked the idea of finally having a deserving vessel for the love she was so eager to give. "My plan?"

"Yes. For selling your half of the apartments."

She wasn't aware she needed a plan outside of getting out her address book and calling her contacts, starting with the wealthiest ones. "I don't really feel like I should share my strategy with you."

"So you don't have one."

He was so arrogant it made her want to scream. And kiss him. Again, confusing. "That's not true. My plans are just more fluid than yours are. It's called being flexible and thinking on your toes. You should try it sometime."

He shook his head, his signature dismissive move. "Being flexible isn't a strategy, it's a coping mechanism. You sell with a strategy. That's the name of the game in real estate. Sell, sell, sell."

Blah, blah, blah. If only he knew that his little lecture on business was like rubbing salt in the wound. She didn't need constant reminders of how he lived and breathed his job. She was collateral damage from the importance of Michael's career.

"You know," he continued, "if you need some help networking, I host a party every year on December twenty-third. I invite other agents, potential clients. Usually some pretty big hitters. I always get a great turnout. I think people enjoy avoiding their families at the holidays."

"Is that what you do? Avoid your family at Christmas?" Michael had never talked about his family when they were a couple, however hard she'd tried to get him to do it. She didn't know anything more than he had a brother, and parents who he'd hinted were perfectionists.

"You might say that."

She didn't want to take his help, but it might be good to keep her options open. "I'll think about it."

Michael pulled up in front of the Grand Legacy and put the car in Park.

"It really is a beautiful building." Michael rested his hand on the center console, leaning over her and peering up at the building. He was so close, she could practically count the hairs in his perfectly tended stubble. She had once loved to hold on to his face right before he kissed her. He had no idea, but it was her way of reminding herself that Michael Kelly actually wanted to make out with her. The man was an Olympian, as shrewd a businessman as there ever was and the finest male specimen she'd had the good fortune to take to bed. She'd wanted to mark the moment and thank the universe.

But that was in the past. And today was all about her future, as well as that of the baby, the two of them on their own. "It is. I love it. I absolutely love it. Which is why I'm going to sell my units before you do. I simply care more." She reached for the door handle.

"Are you challenging me to a race?"

"No," she scoffed, even though she knew very well that she would take extreme glee in selling her apartments before him. She might be forced to take out a full-page ad in the *New York Times*, or at least go to his office, blow raspberries at him and say, "I told you so" a few hundred times. "I'm a grown-up. I'm not racing you."

"Right. I mean, how would we even decide what the prize is?" He bounced his eyebrows at her, his voice so low and husky that she worried she might pass out and knock her head into the dashboard.

"You do your thing. I'll do mine."

"Or I can just tell myself it's a race. To stay motivated."

"What? You can't do that. You need someone else to race you. I refuse to be that person." *Except I already am that person.*

"I'm pretty sure I can do whatever I want."

"You're being ridiculous." It would be just like him to do this. The doorman appeared and opened Charlotte's car door. "I'm going now."

"You're welcome for the ride, neighbor. Oh, and by the way, we're totally having a race."

Fine. I'll just have to figure out a way to beat your sorry butt.

Three

Charlotte stood inside the doorway of her brand-new luxury Grand Legacy apartment, mesmerized by muscles.

"Ma'am, where do you want this?" Chad, the head of the moving crew she'd hired, blew his sandy blond surfer-dude bangs from his forehead. His lightly tanned brow glistened with sweat. His biceps bulged through his black T-shirt, which was emblazoned with his company's name: Hunks with Trucks.

Charlotte felt giddy. This was the most fun she'd had in months. "In the bedroom, Chad. Thank you. And please, call me Charlotte." Her voice was high and girlie and exploding with flirtation, and she didn't care in the least how goofy it might make her seem.

"Of course. Charlotte." He smiled and winked at the same time, a talent Charlotte did not possess. Chad was getting a really good tip at the end of the day. As was Marco, the tall one with the megawatt smile, Phil, the one with the nerdy glasses whose side job was as a runway model, and James, the brooding serious one with the mysterious tattoo snaking up his arm.

"I can't believe you hired this moving company," Fran said under her breath when Chad was out of view. "But I'm not sorry you did."

"I figure we're entitled to a little fun. Plus, I hate moving." Charlotte had moved thirteen times, more than once a year since she'd moved out of the house at eighteen. That was when her dad had announced that he couldn't "deal" with her anymore—too much sneaking out of the house, and doing things that were unbecoming of a Locke, mostly staying out late and dancing. There was always a lot of dancing.

Charlotte's brothers had done some of the same things, and although their carousing was never on a par with Charlotte's, they were also never reprimanded for it. She despised the double standard and had been glad to go out on her own. She started her party-planning business the next day, and kept at it during her first two years of college, until she eventually flunked out of school and shifted gears out of boredom, the next phase being interior design. "And they're doing a great job." The bonus of hiring Hunks with Trucks was that as a pregnant single woman, these guys might be the only primo male physiques she'd see up close for the foreseeable future.

Fran consulted her watch. "They got here pretty late, though. Aren't you supposed to be done using the freight elevator at two? It's nearly two thirty." She pushed up the sleeves of her pale pink long-sleeved T-shirt. Even helping Charlotte move, Fran was dressed impeccably, like a modern-day Jackie O in slim black capris, flats and pearl earrings.

Charlotte had gone for yoga pants, a camisole and a slouchy T-shirt over that. Her hair had gotten dry shampoo that morning and was pulled back in a ponytail, but she had gone to the trouble of putting on makeup. She was spending part of her day with Hunks with Trucks, after all. She wanted to look good. "I think there are only a few more things for them to bring up."

"Yes, ma'am," Chad said from behind her. "One or two more trips and we'll be out of your hair. The guys are bringing the bigger pieces of furniture up now."

Thor whimpered from his kennel, which had been put in the quietest corner of the living room. Charlotte rushed over to him and poked her fingers between the metal bars. Thor licked her mercilessly with his tiny pink tongue. He wagged his tail so violently that the crate shook. "Sorry, buddy. Just a little longer and I can spring you from jail. I can't let you out when the door's open. I know you and you'll run away." Charlotte turned to Fran. "Let's start getting the plates and glasses unpacked. I have to have something to eat on."

The two made their way to the kitchen, which was over-the-top considering Charlotte's lack of culinary skills, but she loved it nonetheless. Classic white cabinets, white marble countertops, gleaming chrome fixtures and stainless steel appliances, including a six-burner range with a massive hood. She even had a center island, which was practically unheard of in Manhattan, but Sawyer's architect had done an excellent job with maximizing space. Charlotte also had a huge soaking tub in her bathroom, another NYC anomaly, something she was definitely going to break in before the end of the night. The apartments were a new addition to the hotel, as these top floors had been only guest rooms in the hotel's earlier incarnation. It had been Sawyer's idea to bring a residential feel to the building, and Charlotte had to admire her brother's devotion to both carefully restoring the building and not being afraid to try something new. Plus, it meant a business opportunity had fallen into her lap and she was immensely thankful for that.

"I have my first showing on Monday morning," Charlotte said, cutting the packing tape on one of the boxes labeled Glassware. "An old party-planning client. She's newly divorced and got a huge settlement. She wants to move into the city from New Jersey."

"Sounds promising." Fran began helping Charlotte

unwrap the paper around the glasses. "Remind me. How many units do you have to sell?"

"Seven, now that I've bought one. It doesn't sound like a lot, but it'll be a big deal. There's so much competition out there and you have to find the right buyer."

"A person with deep pockets."

"Who also likes the idea of living in a hotel. Sawyer was very specific. He wants resident buyers. He doesn't want absentee owners, so it's a little trickier than simply selling them to anyone with money."

"Well, you could sell it as almost like being in a small building. With only four floors, the residential space is relatively small, and access is closed off from the hotel. That could appeal to buyers."

"Of course, you're sharing the elevators with hundreds of hotel guests."

"You don't have to remind anyone of that. You have a fantastic restaurant downstairs and there will be two bars to choose from once The Cellar is open. You don't get that in most apartment buildings."

"True."

Chad and his big brown eyes appeared in the kitchen doorway. "It seems we have a problem. Another resident was scheduled to move in this afternoon. He's demanding his time with the service elevator and wants to talk to you."

The other resident could only be one person. *Mi-*

chael. To her knowledge, no other units had been sold. "Where is he?"

"He's down the hall, arguing with my guys."

Charlotte glanced at Fran. "I'll be back." Reminding herself to stay calm, Charlotte marched down the hall, Chad in her wake. She could hear men's voices before she rounded the corner to the main stretch, where the elevator bank would be visible. Michael's voice, a sound she had once loved, was the loudest.

When she turned, he was standing there, pointing into the elevator. "You guys have to turn the sofa on its side or it's never going to come out." He caught sight of her and simply shook his head. Again with his never-ending dismissiveness. No one was ever as competent as Michael.

She forced herself to smile sweetly. "Problem?"

"These guys have no clue what they're doing. And they won't let me touch your stupid sofa."

Charlotte stepped closer to check out the scene in the elevator. Two of Chad's guys were trying to turn the sofa, but it seemed pretty well wedged in there. "Chad? Can you take charge here? I'm guessing you're enough muscle to make this happen so we can relinquish the elevator to Mr. Kelly."

"You got it, Charlotte." Chad went to work, instructing his men to make some changes in their plan of attack.

Michael simply folded his arms across his broad chest, pacing the width of the hall. He was dressed in jeans and a Boston Celtics T-shirt. She'd always loved it when he dressed down. It was even sexier than him in a suit, which was already out-of-this-world sexy. Perhaps because it made him more approachable, more like an everyday guy. "Nice moving company," he said. "Hunks with Trucks? You've got to be kidding me."

"Don't tell me you're jealous. I didn't think that was possible." He did seem a little green-eyed about the presence of her studly movers. It left her feeling like things were more even between them. She'd stepped out of his car the other day with the distinct sense that he had the upper hand.

"No, Charlie. I'm not jealous."

Just like that, his words cut her down to size. She hadn't heard him call her Charlie in months and it was like a flaming hot poker to the heart. Nobody called her that. It was a nickname he'd bestowed on her, and he rarely used it when they were around anyone else. It'd been reserved for the times when they were alone as a couple. It was such a potent reminder of the reasons she'd been convinced she not only loved him, but that he was also at least capable of falling in love with her. How wrong she'd been. "You could stand to get a sense of humor, Michael. They've been great to work with. Totally professional outfit, top to bottom."

"I think I see the problem," Chad said.

"Oh, good. He thinks he sees the problem." Michael threw up his hands. "You might find them professional, but I have a team of six guys downstairs, waiting to use the elevator, the elevator that I had reserved for two o'clock. You're using up my time."

"I'm sorry. I had no idea you were in such a rush."

"I have a showing this evening. Here."

"Tonight?" Damn him. He was always ahead.

"Yes, tonight. You know I don't waste time."

Yes, she knew all about that. And she hated the way it made her feel like a lesser person.

"I have work to do," he continued. "I can't be standing around here all day waiting for everything to get moved into my apartment." He pointed down to the other end of the hall.

"You mean that apartment, but on the eighteenth floor, right? I was told you bought the corner unit up top. Please don't tell me you're going to be living on the fifteenth floor."

Charlotte's pulse began pounding in her ears. *I haven't even moved in, and I'm going to have to start thinking about moving out.*

Michael was going to have to lie about the location of his apartment. There was no way around it. "I always meant to be on fifteen. It'll be quieter. Those top units are too close to the shared terrace. There will be all sorts of parties up there. I don't want to deal with that." The truth was that he'd asked to have his unit moved to Charlotte's floor. He'd told Sawyer it was because the upper units were primo and would be easier to sell. Hell, he'd told himself the same thing. But the minute he saw Charlotte again today, he suspected that she was the real reason. He was still so drawn to her, but it was an even more pronounced feeling now. Was it because she seemed to despise him so much? Was that what made it so hot? The conversation they were having was a prime example of their incompatibility.

"You're going to be living down the hall. From me." Her voice and expression carried what he could only describe as profound disappointment. Was he really that bad?

"I'm sorry if that's a disdainful idea, but yes."

"Hmm. Okay." She twisted her lips into a kissable bundle. Charlotte made annoyance and anger sexy.

"Got it," one of the movers said, and just like that, the end of the sofa popped out of the elevator.

"Oh, good. Now we can get off Mr. Kelly's naughty list." Charlotte touched Chad the mover's arm with the tips of her slender fingers.

Michael wrestled with the reasons it bothered him so greatly, while trying to ignore Charlotte's sarcastic comment. He had the elevator reserved and she was using his time. She needed to stop acting as though he was being petty.

The movers in the elevator carried the bright turquoise sofa wrapped in a cocoon of clear plastic out into the hall. "Can we give you a lift?" Chad asked Charlotte.

"I'm sorry?" she asked in a voice that rivaled a cartoon princess.

"A ride. Hop on the sofa and we'll carry you down the hall."

She giggled. "Really?"

"Yes, really. We promise we won't drop you. It's fun."

Chad is fun. Good for him.

"Oh. Okay. Great." Charlotte sat on the couch and the men hoisted her into the air. She grasped the sofa arm as surprise and delight crossed her face. They carried her away, Charlotte waving her fingers at him.

At this rate, Michael just wanted them gone. He couldn't stand another minute of Charlotte and the muscle squad.

Time to get back to work. He made a quick call down to his movers, a perfectly normal company called Manhattan Moving, and retreated to his apartment to make a few phone calls while waiting for the first load to arrive upstairs. Without his home office ready, he was forced to set up in the kitchen, his laptop on the counter. His chocolate Lab, Abby, had already made herself at home, stretched out in a sunbeam gracing the living room floor. One of his hopes with now being closer to his office was that he'd have more time to take Abby to the park and out for runs. He had a dog walker, but it wasn't the same. Abby wanted to spend time with him, and he wanted to spend time with Abby. The relationship between dog and master was a simple one, much easier and more symbiotic than most human relationships.

He touched base with three clients about a handful of different properties, including the client who was coming to see the Grand Legacy that evening. The movers were bringing in the first load when he got a call from his younger brother, Chris. They talked or texted almost every day.

"The Islanders won last night," Chris said.

"Sometimes I wish you had a real job so you wouldn't call me in the middle of the day." Michael smiled and leaned back against the kitchen counter. Chris lived in Washington, DC, about twenty minutes from their parents in Maryland. He worked as a lobbyist. As Michael had learned over the last several years, it's pretty easy to get someone to take a meeting with you when you're a former Olympian.

"You owe me five bucks." They were always betting on sports. No longer living in the same house or competing in swimming, it was one way to keep their sibling rivalry going.

"The winning goal was completely bogus. He kicked it into the net."

"Nope. It went off his skate. They reviewed it. A win's a win."

"Fine. I'll pay you when you come at Christmas."

Michael stepped aside as a mover brought several boxes into the kitchen. He pointed at the center island, indicating that was a good landing spot. "I mean, if you still want to come."

"What else am I going to do? Go visit Mom and Dad? I don't think so."

Michael and Chris had been spending Christmas together, but separate from their parents, for six years now. Things had always been difficult with their father. The man had all the warmth of a dark night in Siberia. There was no parental affection, only an intolerance for anything short of perfection. It was one thing when that revolved around swimming. It had helped both Michael and Chris get to the Olympics. It was quite another when it came to one of their sons being on the wrong end of a broken engagement.

"Okay. I'm just saying that I'm fine. I don't want you to feel like you have to come to New York every year and console me."

"Hey. It's not just you. We both sort of lost our parents that day."

Michael did his best to ward off the guilt. Chris had sided with him when Dad went off the rails about Michael's admittedly disastrous engagement party. Mom took Dad's side, which still confounded them both. Their marriage was anything but blissful.

Out of the corner of his eye, Michael saw a small dog rocket through his foyer. Charlotte raced in behind him. "Thor! No!"

"Hey, Chris. I need to run. Talk to you later?"

"Yeah. Of course."

Michael hung up and rushed to investigate. Charlotte's dog was in the living room, straddling a very startled Abby's leg, humping away. "I take it this is Thor?"

Charlotte pulled her dog off Abby and tucked him under her arm, scolding him. "No. Bad dog."

"Does he always do that? Rush into someone's house and try to mate with the nearest canine?" Michael crouched down and showed Abby some love. "I'm sorry, sweets. He woke you up from your nap and everything."

Charlotte blew out a breath. "I'm sorry. He got out of his kennel and bolted down the hall. He's my little Houdini." She lowered herself to the floor and sat with her legs crossed, letting the dogs sniff each other while she petted Abby. "Hi, Abs. Long time, no see." Charlotte had such a sweet side when she chose to let it out, and he'd nearly forgotten what it was like to witness it. It made her even more beautiful, if that was possible. She cast her eyes up at him. "I think they can get along. I swear Thor's not really like this. I think the move has him out of sorts. He can't figure out what's going on."

"It's funny. I've seen so many pictures of him, but you never brought him to my place. It seems strange that I never met him."

Charlotte shot him one of her looks. He'd said the

wrong thing. Again. "Are you serious right now? It wasn't that I never brought him to your place. It's that we always went to your apartment and my dog was never invited. You're lucky I had a lonely retiree living next door to me. Thor spent most of our relationship with my old neighbor."

Michael hadn't really thought about it. It just always seemed easier to meet up at his apartment. "I'm sorry if it seemed that way to you."

"It didn't *seem* that way. It was that way. You never came to my apartment. Not once."

Was that really true? He guessed it was. *Damn.* Michael's phone rang again, saving him from the onslaught of shame Charlotte was likely about to launch at him. He straightened and fished his cell out of his pocket. "It's your brother. Sorry. I need to get this."

"It's Sawyer? Why would he be calling you?" Charlotte seemed once again miffed by Michael's existence on the planet.

"Maybe because we're working together?" Michael pressed the button to pick up the call. "Hey there, Sawyer. What can I do for you this afternoon?"

"Nothing, actually. This call is purely social. I wanted to know if it's best to mail you something at your office or if you're ready to start getting mail at the Grand Legacy."

"What sort of something?"

Michael watched as Charlotte attempted to further acquaint the dogs by placing Thor back on the floor. Unfortunately, the little brute returned to his previous libidinous activity.

"Is he fixed?" he whispered to Charlotte.

"Yes." She frowned at him.

"I want to send you an invitation to my wedding," Sawyer said.

"Oh. Great. I'd love to come to your wedding." Michael said it entirely for Charlotte's benefit, although he wished he could've received this invitation earlier, when Gabe had been bragging about it.

Charlotte's face made the very short trip from shock to horror.

"It's in a week, and I know this is last minute, but it occurred to me after we met the other day that we're working on this project together and you're the first resident of the Grand Legacy who isn't related to me. I'd like to include you that day if you're free. We're having the ceremony and the reception at the hotel, so you won't have far to go. And, of course, you should feel free to bring a date."

Michael hadn't been on a date since Charlotte had broken up with him. Not that he hadn't entertained the idea. There were several women he'd considered asking out. But something stopped him, every time. He just wasn't sure what his problem was. "Sounds great. You can go ahead and put me down with a plus-one. I'll definitely bring a date." Michael watched for Charlotte's reaction, which turned out to be an overblown eye roll.

Michael and Sawyer said their goodbyes, and the movers brought in another round of boxes along with a few smaller pieces of furniture.

Charlotte scooped up her dog again. "So you're bringing a date to my brother's wedding? Or did you just say that for my benefit?"

Maybe. "Yes and no."

"It wasn't payback for Hunks with Trucks?"

He could admit to himself that he'd been irked that she'd hired an all-male revue to move her into the building, but he wasn't about to own up to it with her. "I don't bother with payback, Charlotte. You're free to do whatever you want. You broke up with me, remember?" He disliked the tone in his voice, the one that said it still bothered him. He knew he should be over it by now, but it still felt like there was a lot unresolved between Charlotte and him. Being around her only brought it to the surface, like scratching a wound that hadn't healed.

"I broke up with you because you practically dared me to do it. Which is probably why we should just agree to be kindly neighbors and work adversaries."

Was that where this was going to end? It seemed a shame, but all signs pointed to yes. And maybe that was for the best. "It doesn't have to be that way."

"So says the guy who insists we're racing to see who can sell their apartments first."

"We're still doing that."

She closed her eyes and sucked a deep breath through her nose. "Goodbye, Michael."

"'Bye." He watched down the hall as she walked away, unable to ignore how much he loved the sway of her hips in stretchy black pants. He was definitely going to need to find a date for her brother's wedding. There was no telling who Charlotte would show up with—probably Chad from Hunks with Trucks.

No, it was time for Michael to get back on the horse and start dating again. Maybe it would help him finally get Charlotte out of his system.

Four

Charlotte's new apartment, especially her home office, was shaping up nicely. Her desk, one of her favorite pieces of furniture, was a floor model she'd picked up for a steal at a lovely designer shop in SoHo. It had weathered gray wood and legs that were heavy and scrolled, with a glass top for smoother writing. She'd never liked the idea of a rolling desk chair—too many opportunities to sit and miss—so instead, she used an upholstered side chair in linen with dark legs and nail-head trim. With a lovely bank of windows streaming in daylight, it was the sunniest possible spot to get her life back on track.

Primped by 9:00 a.m. and dressed for the day in

a knee-length navy skirt, black-and-white checked blouse and black pumps, she sat at her desk and began to plan out her day. It was almost enough to make her feel like a confident and accomplished business-woman. The only thing nagging her was the distinct sense that the clock was ticking. It would only be another ten days or so until she was starting her second trimester.

The words alone—*second trimester*—filled her with a cocktail of excitement and worry that far surpassed any bout of anxiety she'd ever had to battle. She couldn't spend too much time perched on this feather-stuffed chair in her photo-spread-ready office, casually writing herself notes. Soon a crib would need to be added, a rocking chair, a bureau for the baby's things. After that, she'd be focused on practicing breathing techniques and the best ways to navigate her environment while her belly was the size of a Smart car. Soon after that she'd be wandering the apartment in slippers and pajamas, holding her sweet little bundle, wondering what day it was and whether her breasts could ever again be used for anything fun. Or at least that was what Fran had said.

Fran had also been regularly reminding her that she only had a few more weeks before it'd be impossible to walk around in an outfit like the one she was wearing today. At some point soon, some unwitting stranger or member of the hotel staff was going to ask when she was due. Unless she wanted to blame her expanding waistline on late-night potato-chip binges, there was no getting around it. She'd have to start telling people about the baby.

Today was December 15. Ten days until Christmas, when their faction of the Locke family would be spending the holiday at Sawyer's apartment, right before he and his wife-to-be, Kendall, would be leaving for their honeymoon. If she'd sold her half of the units, she would tell them then. Visions of opening gifts before a roaring fire, sipping eggnog and enjoying family time popped into her head. What a lovely backdrop for the announcement that not only Sawyer and Kendall would be bringing a new Locke into the world, but Charlotte would be as well. She imagined good wishes, warm embraces and wide smiles. That was the response she wanted more than anything, and she knew very well that she'd have to live with the memory forever, so she'd better do her best to make it a good one. As far as she was concerned, news of a baby, no matter the circumstances, should be greeted with nothing less than pure joy.

Which was precisely the reason she had not yet told Michael. There was no telling how he would take the news, or if he would take it at all. Knowing him, he'd probably blow it off and say he had to get to a meeting with a client. She wanted to believe there was a chance he'd be open to it once he actually heard the news, but she was haunted by the things he'd said when they were together. Things like *I've never wanted to be a parent. Mine seemed to hate it.*

Charlotte's phone rang, and the caller ID said it was Sawyer. She guessed he was calling to make sure she was actually doing something productive and real-estate-related today.

"Morning, Sawyer. How are you?" she answered.

"Wow. I forget how chipper you can be in the morning."

Charlotte had always been a morning person, which was admittedly incongruous with her party-girl past. She'd never been the type to sleep until noon, even when she was a teenager and had tip-toed her way back into the house at 4:00 a.m. "I've got work to do. Phone calls to make. Luxury condominiums in the most beautiful hotel in Manhattan to show off."

Sawyer laughed. "So it's going well?"

"Great. Fantastic." Charlotte didn't hesitate with her answer, even when she knew she was only putting polish on her unproven sales skills. "I've got my home office all set up. I'm ready to sell."

"And you're okay with the Michael Kelly situation? You seemed tense around him. Is there something I should know?"

Oh, sure. You got two hours to sit down and listen to your sister spill her guts? She sucked in a deep breath and blew it out. The simplest explanation was the best for now. Sawyer would only think less of her if he knew that she and Michael had been romantically involved. She could hear it now. *Is there a single guy in Manhattan you haven't dated?* "I interviewed with his agency earlier this year. He declined to take me on as an agent."

"Oh. Wow. I had no idea. I'm so sorry. That had to have stung a bit."

There it was, that familiar sound—pity. Charlotte wanted so desperately to erase that conditioned response from her family's repertoire. "It's fine. You know. It's just business." She could give herself the it's-just-business answer one thousand times and she still wouldn't believe it. Michael's ability to turn her down for a job and still end up her boyfriend was a shining example of just how often and how easily the man got whatever he wanted. He always won. Always.

"You're right. Sometimes business decisions are nothing more than that. I just wanted to make sure there wasn't any romantic history there."

Charlotte had to think fast. Eventually, her family would know about the pregnancy. Eventually, they would learn that although they were not together, Michael was the father of her child. There was no getting around that. "There's a little romantic history, but it's old news. Done and gone."

"What does 'a little romantic history' mean?"

"It means exactly what it sounds like. A little romance, and it's history."

He blew out an exasperated breath. "I just need to know that there's nothing going on between you two. It's not good for business."

"You realize you sound like a total hypocrite right now?" Much of Sawyer's history with his fiancée, Kendall, involved blurring the lines between business and pleasure.

"I know. But I'm also thinking about the reality of the situation. My romance with Kendall messed up a lot of things for her professionally. She nearly lost her job. It's a double standard, and it isn't right, but oftentimes women are judged for these things differently than men."

He wasn't wrong. Women were judged for *a lot* of things differently than men. "Michael Kelly is in the past, I promise. Nothing to worry about."

"Okay. I just want to make sure everything is aboveboard. I want people talking about the hotel and keeping its reputation as a destination, not gossiping about the agents selling the units. I also want to keep the chance of working with Michael open. I don't want him thinking a single bad thought about a member of the Locke family."

Too late. "Got it. Loud and clear."

"I want you to know I gave the same speech to Noah. It's not just you."

"You did?"

"He has a crush on Lily, our admin. I keep telling him to back off, but he has a hard time keeping the flirtation in check. They're close friends, which makes me nervous enough. I'm amazed he hasn't managed to figure out a way to make a move on her without making me mad."

"What if she's the one for him?"

"For Noah? You know how he is. He'd get restless. She'd quit. There's just too much opportunity for things to go wrong. Kendall and I gambled and it worked out, but it almost never does."

As if Charlotte needed a reason to stay away from Michael romantically—Sawyer would be greatly displeased. Knowing this only confirmed how sensible her plan was. It was best to wait until her units were sold before telling her family about the pregnancy. No more conflict of interest, and she'd also be past the twelve-week mark. Too many pregnancy books insisted it was best to wait until then. "Look. I swear to you that this is a nonissue. Michael and I work in the same industry and we are professionals. I will sell my units and that's all you need to know. Don't you worry." *Leave that up to me.*

"You're very resourceful and there's no doubt you're determined. I know you won't let me down."

Charlotte would deserve every ounce of guilt to come if she let down Sawyer. That's why she wasn't going to let it happen. She glanced at the time on her laptop. "I actually have a showing in a few minutes. I should probably head down to the lobby to meet my client."

"Absolutely. Don't let me hold you up."

"Love you, Sawyer."

"Love you, too."

Charlotte hung up, ducked into the bathroom, brushed her teeth and checked her hair. It was time to kick some butt and charm her way into convincing the New Jersey divorcée to buy her own little piece of the Grand Legacy.

Downstairs in the lobby, Charlotte stood near the concierge desk, trying to stay out of the way as a flurry of people milled about. Folks were checking in, some were checking out and the staff catered to their every need. The holidays were always a very busy time in the city and popular with tourists. If any city knew how to do Christmas, it was New York. Between ice-skating in the shadow of the big tree at Rockefeller Center and the extravagant department-store windows and decor, there was no shortage of cheer. The city had even gotten a dusting of snow last night, although it had been meticulously cleared from the sidewalk in front of the hotel. No detail at the Grand Legacy was ever overlooked.

The lobby itself was tastefully decorated with thick swags of fresh pine garland, adorned with strands of glimmering silver and scarlet beads and studded with tiny twinkling lights. The tree, twelve feet tall and dressed with an array of glass ornaments, was tucked into an alcove next to the sweeping grand staircase, which led to the second-floor speakeasy. Christmas was most certainly coming. As was Charlotte's baby.

In through the revolving door came Charlotte's client, Marie Stapleton, bundled up in a black wool coat and a Burberry scarf. Her face lit up when she caught sight of Charlotte. They rushed toward each other and embraced.

"Marie. It's so good to see you. Let me help you with your coat." Marie had been one of Charlotte's most loyal clients when she had her party-planning business. Marie's husband, or now ex-husband, was a Wall Street bigwig, and they had thrown some seriously over-the-top bashes out at their estate.

"You look lovely, Charlotte. Are you doing something new with your makeup? Your skin looks incredible." Marie unwound the scarf from her neck and worked her way out of her coat, both of which Charlotte took from her.

Charlotte shrugged. "Nope. Same old thing. Maybe I'm getting more sleep?"

"Well, whatever it is, it's working."

Charlotte flagged one of the bellhops, who hustled over to them. "Can you check Ms. Stapleton's things in the coatroom, please?"

"Yes, Ms. Locke. Of course." He smiled and was on his way.

"Shall we go pick out your new apartment?" Charlotte asked. It was such a sales-y thing to say. It was the sort of thing Michael would say. Charlotte was proud of herself for having the nerve to presume that Marie would end up living here.

"I can't wait to see it," Marie replied as they managed to catch the elevator before the doors closed. "I'm dying to be back in the city and I wouldn't mind having you for a neighbor. Think of all the fun we could have. Two single girls, out on the town."

Charlotte smiled and nodded, even though she knew she'd have to hold off on revelry with Marie for at least a year or two unless Marie's idea of "out on the town" included newborns and strollers. They rode up to the fifteenth floor to look at the first unit Charlotte had to offer.

Marie only took a few steps into the foyer before she turned to Charlotte and said, "I'm in love already."

"You are?" Charlotte asked, quickly correcting herself. "Well, don't fall too quickly. There are other fish in the sea, most notably the top-floor units. If you're interested in looking." She flipped on the dining room lights, which included a gorgeous chandelier and four elegant wall sconces.

Marie nodded intently, looking all around the room. "It's beautiful. I can see myself throwing intimate dinner parties here. I'll invite all my single friends and we'll laugh and drink too much wine and talk until the wee hours." Marie painted an appealing picture. Charlotte committed her words to memory—she could use them on a future potential buyer if they weren't as much of a visionary as Marie. "Show me more. Then I definitely want to see one of those top-floor units."

"Yes. Of course. They're more expensive. And in fact, they're a bit outside the price range you gave me." Charlotte knew that many real-estate agents would wait until the client couldn't imagine living anywhere else before they broke the bad news that the price exceeded the budget. But she wasn't most agents. "The units are so new there isn't much room for negotiation, unfortunately."

Marie trailed into the kitchen and gasped when she saw the stunning white marble countertops. She smoothed her fingers over them. "I'm guessing they're worth every penny."

An hour later, Charlotte had given Marie the tour of three units. Now they were settling into a corner booth at the hotel restaurant, which hadn't been ready at the time of the grand reopening and had only been open for a few days. As it was midmorning, Charlotte ordered them a big pot of tea and a basket of handmade pastries. She was starving. "Well? What did you think?" she asked, scarfing down a ginger-blueberry scone in as ladylike a fashion as possible.

"I think the hardest part is going to be picking the unit. They all have different things to fall in love with. The terrace on the top floor is hard to beat, but I love the bathroom configuration in the first one we saw." She sipped her tea and tapped her fingers on the table.

Charlotte's pulse started to pick up. She'd closed appallingly few real-estate deals in her short tenure as an agent. She was still learning the art of reading people when it came to this. There had been several times when she'd worked with someone for weeks, certain they were going to buy at any moment, only to eventually discover that they weren't serious or simply weren't able to make up their mind.

"I don't think you can go wrong, if that helps at all." It was the most diplomatic thing Charlotte could think to say. "It's going to be awesome no matter what you decide. The world is your oyster, and anyone would kill to have the sort of options you do." She blanketed Marie's hand with hers. "Just envision your fabulous new life and where you'd like to be living while you embark on your new beginning."

Marie turned to Charlotte and a tiny tear rolled down her cheek. "You know, I never thought I would be here. I really thought that Bradley and I had one of those marriages that would last."

Oh, no. Charlotte had said something wrong and now she was going to pay the price. "Of course you did. A bright and optimistic person like yourself believes in love. You'll find it again. I know you will. But you won't find it until you're ready to start your new chapter."

"You really think I will?"

"I do. There's no doubt in my mind." It wasn't a line simply to close the deal. "You're sweet and generous. You're smart and a good person. You are truly beautiful, inside and out." Charlotte's entire worldview revolved around people like Marie finding their soul mate. If Charlotte didn't believe with every fiber of her being that someone as wonderful as Marie would find love again, what was there to believe in?

"Okay, then. I'm ready to make an offer." She cut open a muffin and slipped a generous pat of butter inside.

"On the first unit?"

She smiled with a devilish gleam in her eye. "Oh, no. On the top floor."

Charlotte matched Marie's grin with one of her own. *Take that, Michael. Take that.*

Five

After only a few days living in the hotel, Michael already liked coming home to the Grand Legacy. His apartment wasn't quite settled yet, but he was happy, albeit still unsure if living in such close proximity to Charlotte was a good idea. If he was supposed to be the guy getting her out of his mind, having her so nearby wasn't going to help.

Tonight, he had the elevator to himself, which was an unexpected bonus. He leaned against the wall during his ride upstairs. He'd had such a crazy nonstop day, no moment of silence was taken for granted. When he reached his floor and the doors slid open, he got another surprise—Thor, then Charlotte, whizzing past.

He stepped out into the hall, watching Charlotte scurry after her dog while wearing heels. How he loved the sway of her hips in that skirt. "Hey, neighbor. Did Trouble make a break for it again?"

"Very funny calling him Trouble."

"It's only fitting."

Charlotte cornered Thor and scooped him up into her arms. "Bad dog," she scolded, her brows drawing together. The reprimand was followed by kisses on the nose and a ruffling of his ears. If Michael's dog, Abby, was spoiled, Thor was spoiled rotten. "I don't know what his problem is. He's still behaving like a puppy. I thought he would've outgrown this by now."

"Maybe he just doesn't like being cooped up all day. Maybe he needs a walk. I have to take Abby out if you want to go together." He wasn't sure it was a good idea, especially since he'd convinced himself the other night that moving on from Charlotte was his best course of action, but he'd already extended the invitation.

She arched both eyebrows at him. "That sounds like a social outing."

"You can wear a disguise if you're worried someone might see you with me. Sunglasses and a fake mustache, maybe?"

She swatted him on the arm. "That's not what I meant." She pursed her lips and drew in a deep breath through her nose, looking at Thor, not him. "It's just so civilized. Almost like we like each other."

"We do like each other, don't we?" He did his best not to sound hurt by her statement. He loved their biting back-and-forth and never thought of it as genuine dislike. He'd assumed she felt the same way.

"Not always we don't."

"Don't be ridiculous. Even when we argue, it still feels like we like each other. Even when you were breaking up with me, I felt like half of the anger you directed at me was out of affection."

It was true. And maybe that was why he was still so drawn to Charlotte, even when he knew that if he dared to try again, it would be no easy task. She wasn't the type of woman to let him off the hook about anything. It was both her appeal and her downside. He loved a challenge, but only when he had an excellent chance of winning. There was no winning with Charlotte when they each wanted radically different things.

She shot him another doubting look. "I'd say it was more out of affection for the idea of screaming at you."

"It's still attention, darling. I'll take what I can get from you."

"Oh, please. You get all the attention you need and more. Every time I see you, I'm surprised a gaggle of women aren't following you like stray puppies."

"Is that what a group of women are called? A gaggle? Like geese?"

"It's better than calling them a murder, as in a murder of crows."

"True. Gaggle is much more kind." He pulled back the sleeve of his wool overcoat and consulted his watch. It was nearly seven thirty. He really needed to start working less and getting home earlier. "Are we going for that walk or what?"

Charlotte bounced Thor in her arms. "What do you say, buddy? A walk with Abby?"

"Just no canine fornication, mimed or otherwise."

"I'll have to change." She looked down at herself, and her blouse flopped back, revealing the line of her collarbone. Maybe it was the way the light in the hall was hitting her skin, maybe it was the fact that he was lonely and tired or maybe it was that Charlotte had an inexplicable hold on him. That one innocent vision sent his imagination flying off on all sorts of tangents, each involving his clothes and hers mingling on the floor of his bedroom.

"Meet back here in five?" He cleared his throat if only to right his mind.

"Make it ten." With that, she sauntered toward her apartment, skirt in full sway.

He keyed into his apartment. Abby was waiting for him at the door, wagging her tail and following his every move through the foyer. "Hold on, sweets. I need a minute." He dropped his keys on the hall table and hung up his coat and laptop bag. The trip to his bedroom to change into track pants and a sweatshirt was quick. He grabbed his black fleece jacket and clipped on Abby's leash. The forecast was for snow this evening, so he grabbed a hat and gloves, too. He'd learned that Abby had no patience for wearing a dog sweater, but that was probably because she liked to walk at a clip and that kept her body temperature up.

They met Charlotte and Thor at the elevator. She'd changed into jeans and boots, wearing the blue wool coat she'd been wearing the other day when they were at Sawyer's office. It did the most amazing things for her eyes—they were always a rather piercing blue, but now they were even more vivid and breathtaking.

They rode the elevator while the dogs sniffed each other, Thor waging the most eager inspection. Despite the more negative parts of his history with Charlotte, he did appreciate that they could be quiet together without it growing awkward or painful. The elevator came to its graceful stop on the ground floor, and they walked the dogs through the lobby and out onto the street. The night air was ice-cold and clear, but calm—perfect for a brisk walk. They headed west toward the Hudson River greenway, away from the crowds they'd find if they traveled east toward Times Square.

"Smells like snow." Michael grew up in Maryland, so he'd lived through his fair share of snowstorms.

"I hope so. I love it," Charlotte replied, inhaling deeply. "Which is weird because I generally hate the cold. Maybe it's a Christmas thing."

"I can see that. A reminder of family time and presents under the tree?"

She laughed quietly. "Maybe the part about presents and trees. I avoid most reminders of family time. It doesn't always bring up the best memories."

Many of Michael's family remembrances were unhappy, too. His brother was the only bright spot in most of them. "You and Sawyer seem close. He really put himself on the line when he gave you half of my listings. I could've made it ugly if I'd wanted to."

"You made it a little bit ugly, remember?"

"What? By sticking up for myself and reminding him of what we'd already agreed to? That's not ugly. That's my whole day." Today had been particularly bad. Most of the time, he loved his job. It was the closest he'd get to the adrenaline rush of competition. But today, he'd had to remind himself that he had Abby and this walk waiting for him when he got home. It was the only thing that had kept him going.

"Okay, tough guy. I get it." Charlotte flipped up the collar of her coat as they crossed at the corner to the wide pedestrian-and-bike path along the Hudson River. "As far as Sawyer goes, we're pretty close, but not like he and Noah. Those two are really close, but they had a different childhood than I did. My father always worshipped them. Well, at least until Sawyer inherited the hotel and decided to go against my dad's wishes. Noah sided with Sawyer and that's when things went south. Unfortunately, for me, my relationship with my dad has always been bad."

Michael's father was blustery and intense, not the slightest bit pleasant. He didn't talk about him, though, not even to someone like Charlotte, who he knew quite well. He never saw the point. Discussing him felt like it gave his dad even more power over him. He wouldn't allow that anymore. He'd done his time. "I don't get that, though. You're the only girl. Don't dads love their daughters and want to protect them?"

"Maybe if they aren't the family screwup. My dad seems to view me as nothing more than a liability. Maybe if I was more successful at something he might think otherwise."

Michael remembered how eager Charlotte had been the first time he'd met her, when she'd come in to interview for a position in his agency. He'd never before encountered someone quite so desperate to work for him, although there were a lot of people who would do a lot for a spot on his team. He'd hated telling her no, but he knew from their earliest conversations that he'd struggle to reprimand her or push her to meet her sales quota. There was something about Charlotte that revealed a soft spot in him, one he'd never even known he had before he met her. The idea of delivering bad news to her was duly unpleasant. Probably why he'd merely paved the way for their breakup, rather than pulling the plug himself. He'd figured he'd let her walk away with some sense of control and her pride intact.

"You'll be successful, Charlie. You just need to hit your stride."

"So says the guy who has been hitting his stride since he was ten years old."

She wasn't wrong, but it wasn't as effortless as she made it sound. He hadn't just worked hard, he'd suffered—there was an awful lot of mental anguish wrapped up in succeeding on the highest levels. There were certainly days when he'd wondered if it had all been worth it. The high of those big achievements never lasted, and the crash that followed them was often devastating. "How are things going with your side of our friendly wager?"

"I told you I'm not racing with you. I'll never win."

"First off, you don't know that. Second, something tells me that if you did sell out first, you'd rub it in my face for all eternity."

A sheepish smile crossed her lips. "Okay. Fine. I guess we're racing, but I'm only agreeing to that because I contracted my first unit today. After only one showing, I'll have you know. It's the one time in my life I've had a perfect record at something. It won't last, of course. Somebody's going to bail on me at some point."

"I don't know. These are hot properties. In theory, they should sell themselves."

"I'd like to think I had a little something to do with it."

"I'm sure you did."

"And what about you? Had any luck yet?"

It was an unfamiliar reaction, but he really wanted to deflect. He didn't want to be winning. "Two. But we'll see how it goes. I'd say it's anyone's game at this point."

Charlotte came to a halt. Thor kept going until his leash went taut. He rounded back to her and yipped.

"Everything okay?" Michael asked.

She looked up at the sky for a moment. Now that they were out of the forest of buildings and right by the water, you could at least see a few stars. Not many—there were too many lights for that. The cold had turned her face into an adorable patchwork of bright pink and creamy ivory. "I'm fine. I forget that I'm going up against the inimitable Michael Kelly. There's a reason my brother wanted you selling the condos."

He grasped her arm. "Don't you dare let this discourage you."

"I'm not. It's just…" She again stared off, this time out over the water, an inky mystery in the dark. She was so beautiful it was hard not to stare. But it was about more than her sweet lips or the blush of her cheeks. He'd learned in real estate, a vocation where you must become an expert in observing behavior, that most people lived in either the eye of the storm or the heart of it. Not Charlotte. She somehow managed to inhabit both at the same time. She was iron-clad, and she was a marshmallow. Indestructible on the outside, but impossibly soft to the touch.

He stepped close enough that the white puffs of her breath in the cold reached his cheeks. A snow-flake landed on her nose, instantly melting and leaving behind a shiny spot. He reached out and wiped it off with his glove. "It's just what?" The snow was coming more steadily now, and another flake landed on her, this time on her eyelash. It didn't melt, it just fluttered away when she blinked.

"I don't want to talk about it, okay? I have to stop thinking of every little hiccup as if it's an actual set-back. Sometimes things are just a blip on the map."

She was upset that he was one more unit ahead. He wasn't going to apologize, but at least he knew how she felt. So often in their relationship he'd had a hard time arriving at what she was saying or what she wanted. It was only since running into her at Sawyer's office that he'd started to understand that it might have helped his case if he'd done a better job paying attention.

"You're right. No big deal."

She turned to him and smiled. "Shall we head back? I love the snow, but it's really starting to come down. I'm sure you have other things you need to get to tonight."

The only thing he really wanted to get to was

Charlotte. Standing there in the cold, in the dark, with a front-row view of her beautiful blend of strength and fragility, he wanted nothing more than to get lost in her. And maybe now was the time to test the waters. She wasn't mad at him right now. Or at least not that much.

He poked his hand through the loop of Abby's leash and cupped both sides of Charlotte's face. Her eyes popped wide. Her lower lip dropped. He didn't wait for anything else. His mouth fell on hers, just a delicate brush of a kiss at first, but warmth quickly bloomed between them. The softness of the kiss was a brilliant counterpoint to everything around them— the hard edges of the city, the loud noises, the too-bright lights. She leaned into him, pressed her chest against his, stoking the fire. Heat built as her lips parted and she turned her head to be closer. For an instant, it was like the breakup had never even happened. She was his again.

Until she wasn't.

Charlotte wrenched her lips from Michael and turned away. "No. We can't. We shouldn't." Funny how every word she sputtered contradicted what her body wanted, but she couldn't let him start something she wasn't prepared to finish. The old Charlotte would throw caution to the wind and worry about the consequences later, but with a baby in the mix, she couldn't afford to complicate things with Michael.

Things were going to get messy enough when she finally told him.

"I'm sorry." He reached for her. His breath was jagged, coming out of him in fits and stops.

She could hardly look at him. His face made her want to do foolish things. "You shouldn't have done that. You and I are not a couple. We have no business kissing. It's just going to make things more confusing between us."

"I don't understand what exactly is so confusing. We broke up, Charlotte. Sometimes people get back together."

This was her opportunity to tell him, and the words were tumbling in her mind, but they weren't ready to come out yet. She knew Michael. He thought a romantic dinner set the bar too high. There was zero chance he'd react well to a baby, and she couldn't face the reality of that yet. Plus, with her brother's wedding on the horizon and her need to prove herself to her family a pressing matter, it was easier for everyone if she just stayed mum on the subject. "I know you and that was a let's-have-sex kiss." Good God, it really was a let's-have-sex kiss. And she had to be mad about it. "That was not a reunion. What were you thinking anyway?"

"I was thinking that you're beautiful and I wanted to kiss you."

If anyone knew how to say the right thing at the right time, it was Michael. Charlotte wasn't going to fall for it, though. The old Charlotte would've been fawning all over him. *Oh, Michael, you're so romantic.* She knew that it didn't last with him. If he got a work call right now, he'd take it and not remember what they'd been talking about before he'd picked up the phone. "Well, just stop thinking that. You know we're not right for each other. We want different things. Remember?"

He pursed his lips tightly. "I know. You're right. We do want different things. I'm sorry I kissed you."

There. Now she felt better. Sort of. "Thank you. For apologizing."

He held up his hands in mock surrender. "Yes, ma'am. Whatever you say. No more kissing. I wouldn't want to rock the boat again."

Now she knew why she was so bad at setting boundaries. She hated it. "I really think it's time to head back. I'm freezing." Of course, her lips and some of her more delicate parts were still on fire.

"Yeah. I have some more work to do before bed anyway." He blew out a breath and stuffed his hands in his pockets.

They headed back toward the Grand Legacy, walking in silence. The snow blanketed cars parked along the street and stretches of the sidewalk where no one had walked. Christmas and snow were both in the air and Charlotte had never felt more lonely. If she wasn't pregnant, it would've been easy to keep kissing Michael. She wouldn't have this monumental obstacle to get past. She also wouldn't have the one thing in her future she was truly excited about, the thing that kept her going most days—a baby.

"You know, you still never told me why you went to England." Michael looked down at her, his cheeks ruddy and wind-chapped. They were about a block from the hotel. They needed more ground to cover than that for Charlotte to explain.

"When I said I needed to regroup, it was the truth." She shook her head and concentrated on the sidewalk in front of her, kicking up snow with her boots as she went. "I won't lie, Michael. I felt a little lost after we broke up."

"Huh." He didn't say another word, he just bunched his shoulders up around his ears to ward off the cold.

"*Huh?* What does that mean?"

"I'm just thinking. Give me a minute." He shot her a look that said she needed to back off. "You know, our breakup didn't have to happen. There wasn't any reason we had to rush to get serious, Charlotte. We'd only been together three months. You were the one who was forcing the issue."

Half of a laugh left her lips. They were having two separate conversations and she had too much she still had to keep to herself. *I was forcing the issue because I loved you, you big dummy.* "I really don't want to get into the timing of our breakup." *It'll just break my heart.* "And that's not the only reason I went to England. I needed to decide what my next move was career-wise. It's not a simple thing when you're trying to make a name for yourself in an industry that is essentially a fishbowl and your ex-boyfriend is a great white shark."

Michael stopped at the hotel's revolving door. "You're perfectly capable of standing on your own."

"I know that now. I didn't know it before." Charlotte pushed the brass bar across the glass window. The rush of heat in the hotel lobby was heavenly.

"And I'm not a great white. I'm more of a hammerhead."

They made their way back to the elevator and hopped on board. Abby and Thor were back to sniffing and licking each other. Charlotte wasn't sure how it was so easy for the dogs to figure it out. After all, they'd gone from Thor only wanting sex and Abby fending him off to actually being friends. At this point, friendship was the best-case scenario with Michael, and she had to do everything to steer herself toward that.

"Thanks for the walk," she said when they arrived on the fifteenth floor. "I guess I'll see you around."

"Your brother's wedding is this weekend."

Charlotte nodded, fighting her inner sense of dread. *Please don't bring a date.* "Yes. Definitely that. I'll see you on Saturday."

Six

Charlotte walked into the Grand Legacy speakeasy at 5:15 p.m., for a prewedding cocktail with her brothers. Hers would be nonalcoholic, but she hoped no one would notice. It was Sawyer's idea to close the bar to the public and invite the wedding guests to enjoy a libation before the nuptials. Aunt Fran was in the lobby waiting for her date, an old flame she'd run into outside the hotel a few days ago.

"There's the handsome groom," Charlotte said to Sawyer, finding him standing at the bar with Noah. "How are you holding up? It's a big night."

He gave her a shaky grin, a kiss on the cheek and a warm embrace. Tugging at the collar of his crisp white shirt and straightening the sleeves of his classic black tuxedo jacket, he looked every bit the part of dashing yet nervous groom. "I'm a wreck."

"A happy wreck," Noah said, chiming in. "I told him not to worry. We have security stationed at every exit in the hotel. Just in case Kendall decides to make a run for it."

They all laughed, quite effortlessly she noticed. For a moment, it felt like old times. Noah was always making jokes. When they were kids, he regularly annoyed their father with wisecracks at the dinner table. After their mother had passed away, their dad insisted on eating every meal in the formal dining room at the Locke estate. It had seemed ridiculous and stuffy at the time, but now that Charlotte was an adult, she realized those words—*ridiculous* and *stuffy*—were an apt description of her father.

"You look gorgeous, Charlotte." Sawyer's vision narrowed as he appraised her. "Did you do something different with your hair?"

Charlotte smiled sweetly. Sawyer was as sharp and observant as a person could be, but she'd managed to dodge any pregnancy suspicion. "That's nice of you to notice. I curled it a bit. No big deal."

Sawyer nodded toward the speakeasy entrance. "Michael Kelly's here."

Charlotte was immediately hit with a flash of excitement she wanted to banish from her body. She turned and got her wish. The vision before her zapped whatever stupid part of her brain had decided there was reason her heart should flutter when she heard Michael's name. He'd followed through on his promise to bring a date.

He spotted them and waved, and the pair approached. Michael's companion, she of zero body fat, had a flawless complexion, full red lips, legs that went on forever and jet-black hair so glossy even Charlotte wanted to skim her hands down it.

"Good evening, Locke family." Michael shook hands with Sawyer and Noah, but Charlotte received only a polite nod. It was her fault for having been so adamant about no more kissing—she'd failed to be specific that an affectionate peck on the cheek in the presence of a supermodel would be perfectly acceptable. "I'd like you all to meet Louise." He presented his prize while finishing the introductions.

Charlotte had no choice but to shake the hand of the woman whose butt was in no way acquainted with gravity. "Gorgeous dress."

"Oh, thank you." A perfunctory smile crossed Louise's luscious lips. She was probably tired of fielding compliments all day.

Charlotte berated herself for being generous, especially when she caught the arrogant smirk that crossed Michael's lips. He was so handsome in a tux it made her dizzy—his shoulders were impossibly straight from swimming seven zillion miles over his lifetime, and the black jacket only accentuated the sharp line. He'd worn a traditional tie rather than a bow tie, which made his normally imposing height that much more evident. His hair was perfect, walking that sexy line between impeccably groomed and disheveled.

A waiter came by with a tray of champagne. Michael took two flutes, handing one to Louise. Why that one perfectly appropriate and polite gesture made Charlotte so mad, she had no idea. "No, thank you," Charlotte said to the waiter. She made a mental note to drink an entire bottle of champagne by herself once the baby had arrived and she was no longer breastfeeding. "I'll get something from the bar."

Noah declined as well. "Sawyer and I had better head downstairs to the grand ballroom."

The nervousness returned to Sawyer's face.

Charlotte found it adorable to see her normally unflappable brother so worked up over his wedding day. "Oh, right. You don't want to be late." She kissed him on the cheek. "It's going to be amazing. You'll do great. I love you so much."

"I love you, too," Sawyer said, returning her affection. He and Noah disappeared into the growing crowd in the bar.

Charlotte was now alone with the man who had no earthly idea she was pregnant with his child and the freakishly beautiful woman he would probably end up taking up to his apartment, down the hall from hers, in a few short hours. She should probably sleep with her earplugs tonight.

"Big day for your brother," Michael said.

"Yes," Charlotte replied. She would've said something to continue the conversation, but everything running through her head right now was appallingly impolite. *So, Louise, what's it like living on cucumber slices and ice water?*

"You have the most stunning skin," Louise said, shocking the hell out of Charlotte. "It's like you're glowing."

While putting on her makeup, Charlotte had worried that the pregnancy made her face look more like a moon. Louise's kindness was appreciated, even if it had come out of nowhere. "Thank you."

Louise tugged on Michael's sleeve. "Do you see the way she glows?"

He cast his eyes to Charlotte and their gazes connected like there was nowhere else for either of them to stare. "She's gorgeous. She's always been gorgeous."

Charlotte's heart returned to hyper fluttering. Her breath couldn't find its way out of her throat. She both loved and hated these moments with Michael, especially since they'd become neighbors. Would she ever be able to shrug them off? She couldn't even bear to answer the question. Anything having to do with the future and Michael was a crap shoot at best.

Louise smiled at Charlotte as she took Michael's

hand and rested her head against his shoulder. He looked…well, it was hard to put into words. Uncomfortable, but it wasn't like he was protesting. His hand was curled in at her waist and Charlotte couldn't stop studying his long fingers. Nor could she ignore the fact that if she could have anything at that moment, it would be Michael's hand on her. Charlotte's breaths came faster and she was overcome with a deep desire to take a hunk of Louise's shiny locks in her hand and give a non-gentle pull. *Stop it. He's not right for you.* Michael wasn't hers to fight for, and this was her brother's wedding—she needed to behave herself. That meant the two minutes she'd already endured with these two was enough.

"I'm so sorry, but you'll need to excuse me. I'm going to get something from the bar." She didn't wait for a response before she scurried off. "Club soda with lime, please," she blurted to the bartender. She wondered if it would be weird to strike up a long conversation with him, just so she could tell Michael she was busy if he happened to approach her.

"Gladly, Ms. Locke." He was very efficient, almost too quick. He had her drink to her in no time flat.

"Thank you." She tucked some cash into the tip glass, then turned and nearly ran into the man behind her. "Oh, my gosh. I'm so sorry."

He cocked his head to the side. "You're Charlotte

Locke, aren't you?" He was fairly good-looking, with dark hair, bright white teeth and kind blue-gray eyes.

She nodded. "Guilty as charged."

He held out his hand, but when she offered hers, he raised it to his lips. "Very nice to meet you. Gabe Underwood. I'm in real estate, too."

For a moment, Charlotte hardly knew what to say. A colleague. Someone had recognized her in the context of her profession, not just because she came from the well-known family who owned the hotel. "It's so nice to meet you, too. Are you a friend of Sawyer's?"

"I've done one project with your brothers. I'm hoping we can do more in the future. I really enjoy working with them."

"Oh, nice. I'll be sure to tell them that we met."

"I heard you snatched away half of the condo listings in the hotel from Michael Kelly. You have no idea how happy I was to hear that."

Charlotte was a little surprised she was the subject of industry gossip. It was deliciously exciting. "The family connection didn't hurt."

Gabe shrugged. "Doesn't matter. All that matters is that you left a chink in Michael Kelly's armor."

Charlotte glanced over at Michael. He made eye contact with her, then slowly shook his head and mouthed the word *no*. As to what that meant, Charlotte didn't know, but she could guess that he didn't like her talking to Gabe. She hooked her arm in his. "Were you going to get a drink?"

"Yes. Can I get you anything?"

Charlotte tossed back her head and laughed. She was mad at herself for wanting to make Michael jealous, but she couldn't help it. "No, thank you. I'm fine."

Gabe got his drink and was back at her side in a flash. He was nothing if not attentive. He cradled a glass of something suitably manly—brown liquor of some sort in an old-fashioned glass with a single ice cube. "So, I have at least one buyer who might be interested in one of the units here in the hotel."

"Oh, really?" Charlotte was starting to like Gabe more and more.

"Young couple. Married three years. He works in advertising, and she's in fashion. They have a two-year-old son and have been living in Connecticut, but they're both ready to be closer to work."

"Sounds like the Grand Legacy could be a good fit. Sawyer is dead set on resident tenants."

"Would early next week work for a showing? You'll have to let me know what your schedule is like."

"I'll work around whatever works for your clients. Evenings are fine if that suits them best."

"Perfect. I'll need your number, though. I don't think I have it." Gabe slid her a sly smile and took a sip of his drink. He wasn't as smooth as Michael, but he wasn't that far off.

Charlotte was thrilled to dig her business card out of her evening bag and hand it over, especially when she could feel Michael's eyes on her. She smiled at Gabe and remained focused on their conversation as they discussed the state of affairs in upscale Manhattan housing. Charlotte did more listening and taking mental notes than contributing, but she figured she had to start somewhere. She was quickly learning two things—real estate in New York, especially in the upper tier of high-priced residential properties, was cutthroat, much more so than she'd really understood. And the other new bit of info was that Gabe did not like Michael, and he maintained that most other agents didn't, either. That part definitely put her in a peculiar spot. However much she and Michael were working in opposition, the bottom line was that she disliked hearing other people speak ill of him.

A female bartender stepped out from behind the bar and clinked a champagne glass with a spoon several times. The chatter in the room softened. "The grand ballroom is now open if everyone would like to make their way downstairs. The ceremony will begin in thirty minutes."

The rumble of conversation resumed to its previous noise level, and guests began to file out of the bar. Charlotte wasn't ready to give up the comfort of having a companion. "I'm up front with family if you'd like to join me," she said to Gabe.

His eyes were wide with surprise. "I would love it. Thank you so much."

There. Now she wouldn't have to feel so bad about

Michael and his date. They followed the flow of guests out of the speakeasy, down the grand staircase and around to the ballroom. Inside, they filed up the aisle and took their seats on Sawyer's side in the first row. The ballroom looked splendid, lights dimmed and there were plenty of candles everywhere. Sawyer had been specific about wanting a small ceremony, so there were fewer than one hundred seats. A gorgeous art deco arch had been erected, covered in white calla lilies. Tables for the reception ringed the room, with elaborate but tasteful centerpieces in an elegant color scheme of white, silver and gray.

Charlotte's parents had been married in this room. By all reports, it had been an even smaller affair, since Charlotte's mom was pregnant with Sawyer, just like Kendall would soon be having Sawyer's baby. She wondered how her mom had felt that day. Charlotte didn't really have any warm memories of her parents as a couple. They'd never been affectionate around her, or not that she could remember. She only had sweet remembrances of her mom, and those were hazy at best, worn away by time. Charlotte had been only seven years old when her mother died.

Gabe's phone beeped with a text. "I'm so sorry. I should've muted my phone."

Charlotte touched his arm. "It's okay. Answer it if you need to."

"I'll just be one second." Gabe discreetly walked to the end of their row.

Aunt Fran arrived with her date, a dashing man with a thick head of salt-and-pepper hair. "Charlotte, this is Phil. Phil, this is my favorite niece, Charlotte."

They shook hands. Phil had a killer smile and a firm grip. *Way to go, Fran.*

"Do you mind leaving a seat for my friend, Gabe?" Charlotte nodded in his direction.

Fran cocked an eyebrow and left the seat to Charlotte's left open. "Where'd you find this one?"

"He's another real-estate agent. We were chatting in the bar."

Fran nodded and looked back over her shoulder. She closed her eyes and shook her head. "Oh, no. Your father actually showed up."

"He did?" Charlotte turned to the back of the room. Sure enough, her dad was holding court with his current wife, Catherine. They were greeting several old family friends.

"I probably shouldn't stay," Fran said. "Or I should at least move back a row or two."

How Charlotte despised the drama created whenever her father showed up. "You don't think he'd make a scene, do you? It's Sawyer's wedding, for God's sake."

"I'm not your father's favorite person. You know that."

Charlotte did know that, but she'd never known the reason why. She suspected it might've been that Fran never liked Charlotte's dad and had not wanted her sister to marry him. After Charlotte's mom died, the rift had grown wider. There had reportedly been an argument at the funeral, but Charlotte was so young, she knew nothing of it. The one time she'd dared to ask Fran about it, her aunt had said that no good would come of discussing it. "I love you. That's all that matters. And Sawyer wants you here. You're not going anywhere."

Fran nodded. She was tough as nails. "You're right. If your father decides to make a stink, I'll have no choice but to put him in his place."

As if that comment had just summoned him, Charlotte's dad appeared, holding hands with Catherine, who said, "Hello, Charlotte," and took the seat next to hers.

Her dad leaned across Catherine's lap. "Nice of you to show up for your brother's wedding."

Look who's calling the kettle black. "I've been back in town for weeks, Dad. You know I wouldn't miss this for the world."

He cleared his throat and crossed his legs. "Oh, that's right. I forget how the three of you are so tightly wound in your allegiance to each other."

Probably because we had to be that way. Otherwise we never would've made it through our childhood in one piece. Charlotte wasn't going to take the bait. If she stopped talking, hopefully her dad would back down, too.

Sawyer and Noah appeared at the archway, as did

the minister. Poor Sawyer looked even more nervous, eyes laser-focused on the back of the room. The music started and everyone stood. Gabe quickly took his place next to Charlotte. "I'm so sorry."

"No problem."

Kendall's one and only bridesmaid marched up the aisle, but all eyes were drawn to the bride, who was smiling wide and waiting her turn. Kendall's father had never been a part of her life, and her mother had passed away a few years ago, so she had chosen to stride up the aisle on her own. She took each measured step carefully, as if she was savoring every minute. Charlotte couldn't blame her. She would do the same and soak up every second of the spotlight, if her big day ever came. Not that she had to worry about it anytime soon. Being pregnant and single severely diminished the dating pool.

Kendall was stunning in a gorgeous bias-cut dress of satin charmeuse. The woman wasn't afraid of showing off her curves, even the four-plus months of baby that made her belly beautifully rounded. The smile on Sawyer's face when she reached the archway filled Charlotte's heart with so much love she could hardly stand it. His shoulders relaxed the instant Kendall took his hand. A tear streamed down Charlotte's cheek. At least her brother could have this.

The ceremony was simply beautiful. Kendall and Sawyer exchanged their vows, staring deeply into each other's eyes. Charlotte kept her hands in her lap, wishing she had someone to hold on to right now, and fought back the idea that this day would be better if Michael hadn't dared to bring a date. Her brother and Kendall exchanged rings, and with the single proclamation from the minister, they put the final touch on their big day with a sweet and tender kiss.

Everyone rose to their feet and applauded. Charlotte's tears were coming faster now, and she wasn't really sure why. She wasn't the type to cry at a happy moment. Perhaps it was the sea of mixed emotions she was swimming in every day—excited by the prospect of her baby, nervous about what her family would think, thrilled that her most recent steps forward in her career had been strong, scared to the bone about what Michael would say when she finally broke the news of the pregnancy.

Charlotte turned to Gabe. "Hug?" he asked, tilting his head to the side.

She accepted his offer. She needed it. "Thank you." She then took a bigger, stronger embrace from Fran. "Happy day, isn't it?"

Fran's cheeks were just as streaked with tears as Charlotte imagined hers must be. "Very, very happy, darling." She then pointed toward the back of the room. "It appears as though your father is leaving."

Charlotte looked to see that her dad and his wife were ducking through the doors, bypassing the receiving line. "What a jerk."

"Are you surprised?" Fran asked.

"Not really," Charlotte muttered. "Although I certainly hoped for better."

They made the trip through the receiving line, congratulating Kendall and Sawyer. Meanwhile, the staff cleared away the chairs from the ceremony and guests consulted the seating chart for dinner. The music became decidedly more celebratory, waiters circulated through the room, offering champagne and hors d'oeuvres.

Charlotte caught Michael's eye again. He was definitely watching her. She didn't have much of an opinion about Gabe, but she was starting to form an opinion of Louise, who was now trying to get Michael's attention. She stood in front of him, poking his chest so forcefully that Michael visibly recoiled.

Louise abruptly turned and pointed at Charlotte, then returned her sights to Michael, waved a hand in his face and stormed off. Michael looked up at the ceiling, then went after her. Charlotte had to quiet her immense inner triumph. The truth was, she felt bad for him. She only enjoyed seeing his ego bruised when she was doing the bruising. Somewhere deep inside her was a soft spot for Michael Kelly that went on for miles.

Seven

Dinner at Sawyer's wedding had been a test, and not merely because Michael's date, Louise, had first needed convincing to return to the ballroom, only to complain extensively about the food. The sight line from Michael's seat meant that he could see Charlotte and Gabe perfectly. He'd had to endure every smile, every instant their shoulders touched, every moment of conversation the pair shared. If Charlotte was putting on a show for his benefit, it was an award-winning performance. She seemed smitten.

Now that the meal had been served, the toasts had been made and the dancing was getting underway, Michael had had enough. He couldn't watch them for another minute. And to think he'd been worried about Chad from Hunks with Trucks. This was far worse. Far. Worse.

Now they were flirting. She was giggling and throwing back her head, touching the lapel of Gabe's jacket. It made Michael want to punch a wall, but only after placing Gabe's face squarely in front of his fist. Charlotte glanced in his direction for an instant. The eye contact, the bolt of blue from twenty yards away, registered first in his chest. She knew he was watching and she didn't care. If anything, she was enjoying it.

Louise grasped his chin and jerked his face to hers. "Are you seriously going to stare at Charlotte Locke again? Because if that's what's going on, I'm leaving. I already put up with it the entire time we were upstairs in the bar, and all through dinner."

He shook his head and did everything he could to focus on Louise, but his eyes were drawn to Charlotte, and he couldn't keep them trained where they were supposed to be, no matter how hard he tried. "I'm not staring. If it seemed like I was, I wasn't." *How lame an excuse could I possibly give?*

"I'm serious, Michael. I would much rather be wearing a pair of yoga pants and drinking a glass of wine than standing in a stuffy wedding reception wearing a dress that I can hardly breathe in." She ran her fingers along the lapel of his jacket. She leaned closer, putting her mouth perilously close to his ear.

"Or, maybe we could go upstairs and you can help me get out of this thing."

Normally, a proposition like that was a no-brainer. Except Michael's conscience couldn't let him do it. He couldn't leave Charlotte alone with a creep like Gabe. She might think he was a nice guy, or funny or charming—the thought made him shudder—but Michael knew for a fact that Gabe was none of those things. He had to save his dear Charlotte. Even if she might stab him in the eye with a cake fork for doing it.

"You know. I gotta be honest. I really need to work the room. There are a lot of potential clients here and I'd be a fool to pass up a chance like this."

Louise's arms hung at her sides like she was carrying pails of water. It wasn't a particularly flattering look. "You're serious. You're turning me down. Right here. Right now."

He needed to end this. "I'm sorry. I'm glad you came to the wedding with me, but I just don't think this is going to work out. I'm happy to call a car service to pick you up or pay for a cab."

She huffed and held out her hand.

Okay, then. Michael fished his wallet out of his back pocket and handed her a fifty-dollar bill, which she sharply plucked from his fingers. Thank goodness they hadn't kissed or anything more. Then he might worry about being arrested for this transaction.

"You're a jerk. Just so you know."

So I've been told. "I really am sorry. Enjoy the rest of your evening."

In a flash, the woman previously known as his date was gone. Now to get rid of Gabe. He marched over to Charlotte and placed his hand at the small of her back. "Hello, Charlotte. Would you like to dance?"

Gabe's eyes nearly crossed. He stepped in front of Charlotte, physically keeping her out of arm's reach. "Hold on a minute, Kelly. I'm with Charlotte. Back off."

Charlotte peeked around Gabe. "Michael. What are you doing? Gabe and I are having a nice time."

"Yeah," Gabe muttered.

"But is he your date?" Michael was already fairly sure of the answer. He just wanted to hear it directly.

This time, Charlotte elbowed Gabe out of the way. "What if he was my date?"

Ah, the rhetorical question. As good as a real answer. "Then I'd tell you that I was surprised and that you are on a date with a bit of a snake." He shot a look at Gabe. "No offense."

"No offense? How am I supposed to be anything but offended by that?" Gabe countered.

"I call 'em like I see 'em. You're always working an angle, Underwood. Something tells me Noah Locke won't be too happy to find out you came to his brother's wedding and proceeded to pick up his sister."

"He didn't pick me up. We were talking business."
Charlotte rolled her eyes.

"See? I didn't pick her up. You can shove off,
Kelly."

"Not until I get an answer from Charlotte about
that dance. If you aren't picking her up, she's free
to dance with any man here. Those are the rules of
wedding etiquette."

"Maybe she just wants you to leave her alone."

Charlotte shot Gabe a look that Michael had been
on the receiving end of a few times. Michael knew
from experience that it was not fun. "Enough. Stop.
I'm going to dance with Michael because he asked.
Then perhaps we can resume our conversation when
I'm done."

Michael knew a lot of things, but one thing he
knew above all else—Gabe was not getting another
shot at Charlotte while he was still breathing and still
in this room. No way, no how.

"I was just trying to be chivalrous." Gabe was
backing down. Michael wished he'd slither back into
whatever hole he'd come out of.

"That's a nice idea, but I don't need to be saved."

What a reversal of fortune in a very short amount
of time. Ten minutes ago, Michael was stewing in his
own juices over being stuck with a woman he didn't
really care about, but who was preserving his ego.
And now Charlotte had given Gabe the heave-ho.

"I don't know that I have ever been more attracted

to you," he said. He cupped her elbow and pulled her to the dance floor.

"So you were serious about dancing? I thought you were just being an arrogant ass."

He pulled her into his arms. "Of course I was serious. I wanted to dance with you."

"Was it really me? Or was it more a case of buyer's remorse over your date?"

Louise had been a mistake he was accustomed to making. He'd appraised her by the way she filled out a dress. He hadn't considered much else. "She's a nice girl. Just not right for me."

Charlotte looked up into his eyes. It was so clear she was searching for more, it felt as if she was trying to pry open his soul, one of the more frightening prospects of time with Charlotte. There were no stones left unturned with her, no matter how hard he tried. "Is there such a thing? A woman's who's right for you?" she asked. The question was even heavier than the words. It felt as though it had lifelong implications.

He sighed and pulled her closer. He couldn't handle another second of that probing look on her face. He wanted to enjoy this time with her, not endure it. "You're the closest I've come." He was surprised he could make the admission, but it was the truth. Charlotte hadn't been the one, but that was only because he was certain there was no such thing. As a couple, they hadn't been perfect together, but they'd been good, and he still wasn't sure why good hadn't been enough to make her happy.

"I suppose I should be flattered by that? I came the closest to cracking the mystery of Michael Kelly?"

"I'm not that hard to figure out, Charlotte. I'm really not."

"You're right. A dead-end road is pretty easy to decipher. At least you know where you stand."

"What do you want me to say? That I regret our breakup? Because I do." The air stood still for a moment, and the song changed, but Michael wasn't about to let go of her. If anything, he pulled her closer. He dropped his head toward hers as well, just to draw in her sweet fragrance.

"If you regretted it, why didn't you try to fix it? Why didn't you come after me?"

"You just told Gabe you don't need to be saved."

"I don't. But that doesn't mean I wouldn't have appreciated the gesture."

Michael laughed quietly. He'd never understand the logic behind jumping through hoops for show, especially when you had a reasonable expectation that it wouldn't pay off. "I thought about it, but the next thing I knew, you were in London. That seemed like a pretty obvious answer to me. I wasn't about to go after you in England."

"I always planned to come back."

"Is that why you didn't say goodbye?"

"I really didn't think you cared enough to notice."

Now the thought that had made him laugh seconds earlier only made him sigh. Should he have gone after her? Should he have fought for her? He'd never done it before and he wasn't sure he had the wherewithal to double down on a relationship. You go after a woman, you beg her to take you back, that comes with expectations of commitment. At the very least, you open yourself up to conversations about where things are going and how things are going to work. He had so little confidence in love it was impossible to imagine ever doing that.

"I cared, Charlotte. I really did. However much you think I didn't, I did." Could he say what was waiting at the back of his throat and buried deep in his head? Was he really willing to start something with Charlotte again? She'd said point-blank the other night that there would be no kissing between them, that they had no business being together. So should he try anyway? It would be no easier the second time. If anything, knowing her, she'd make things harder. "And if it makes anything better, I made a mistake when I let you go. You have to believe me when I say that."

Charlotte gazed up into Michael's eyes, his words triumphantly ringing in her ears like church bells in a tower. *I made a mistake when I let you go.* She couldn't decide which part of the statement she liked most, but there was a strong contender for first place. "A mistake?"

He nodded, not shying away from it. "I'm not an idiot. I can admit to it when I mess up. You were jumping the gun all that time we were together, but maybe I did the same thing." He focused intently on her. "Maybe we need to switch to a lower gear and see where that takes us."

Goose bumps raced up Charlotte's arms. Michael's voice had dipped to a deep, gravelly place that made her spine feel like it was made of rubber. His lips parted slightly. Hers mirrored the motion. She wished she could rewind the events of the other night and rescind the moratorium on kissing. "Have any thoughts? About where that should take us?" She knew very well what she was starting, but Michael's admission that he'd made a mistake had her second-guessing every conclusion she'd ever reached about him.

The sexiest smile rolled across his face. "I have lots of thoughts, Charlie. Not sure I should say them out loud in the middle of your brother's wedding reception. This is a fairly G-rated event."

"So we should go somewhere more private?" She licked her lips in anticipation of what he might say next.

"You kill me when you do that, you know. The lick-lipping thing."

Heat rushed to her cheeks. "I do?" No one had ever

squeezed so much coquettishness into two syllables before. She was proud of herself.

"Yes. It makes me feel left out." His words made everything in her body go warm, a good ten-degree spike at least. "As for your suggestion that we go somewhere private, yes. I think that's smart."

Charlotte slyly glanced across the dance floor. Sawyer was too caught up in Kendall's eyes to notice a thing. "Yes. Now."

They walked double-time out of the ballroom and down the hall to the elevators. Charlotte's mind was running on adrenaline, which was enough to make her feel drunk, even when she was stone-cold sober. Two more people joined them for the ride upstairs, meaning there could be no touching. Charlotte was dying. That kiss the other night had not been enough. It had taken her twenty-four hours to shake it off. She just wanted more of Michael, now. The other riders got off on the twelfth floor, but that didn't give them much time. Charlotte flattened him against the wall of the elevator, popped up onto her tiptoes and pulled his lips down to hers. They hardly got started when the doors slid open.

"My place?" he asked, tugging her in that direction.

This had been an issue when they were together, but she didn't have the strength to argue now. "Sure." As they made their short trip, in the brief flashes when her brain was working, all she could think was

that she should not be going to Michael's apartment.
Not now, when night had fully fallen and they had
just spent too much time pressed against each other
on the dance floor. The heat was still present from
his hand in the curve of her lower back. The tingles
were still there from that moment when he'd looked
into her eyes and told her that he thought he might
have messed up. But she couldn't get past one burning question—had she been wrong about him?

"Drink?" Michael asked as he opened the door
and they stepped inside.

Charlotte wandered over to the windows on the far
side of his apartment, if only to steal a moment and
make sure she really wanted this. "Just some water,
thank you. I've had my fill." She'd been drinking
club soda with lime all night, but she hadn't said a
thing when someone suggested it might be a gin and
tonic. She simply hadn't let anyone get her a drink
from the bar during the entire wedding. She'd gone
so far as to sneak off for a champagne flute of ginger
ale when it came time to toast.

"Good." His voice was right behind her, and before she could turn around, his hands were on her
shoulders and his body heat was once again pouring
into hers. "I don't want a drink, either." His thumbs
caressed her shoulders, his fingers pressing into the
flesh of her arms.

Tiny zaps of electricity sizzled over the surface of
her skin. She sensed what was coming and she knew

that she should say no, but she didn't want to. Michael was too much of a sexy, handsome package to deny herself any longer. Even when she worried that she might be nothing more than his prey, she was more than willing. She'd missed this so much. She wanted this with everything she had.

He dipped his head lower and his lips brushed her neck, his stubble scratching her. That sliver of pain put her on notice that this was happening. In the window, she could see their reflection. It was a dreamy shadow, hard edges smudged, dotted with raindrops on the glass. His hair fell forward as he kissed her neck, his mouth now open, his warm tongue making her lose her mind. It felt so good she wanted to close her eyes and languish in every heavenly sensation, but she loved watching him focus on her. For that moment, she seemed like she might be everything to him, precisely what she had once hoped to be.

He hooked his thumbs into her dress straps and pulled them down her shoulders. He gathered her hair in one hand and kissed his way across her back, sending waves of tingles along her spine. His lips weren't just warm, they were on fire. His kiss was urgent. Like he needed to get somewhere. He pressed his long body against hers, his knees met the back of her thighs, his chest met her shoulders and what she could only guess was his rock-hard erection met the small of her back. She pushed right back into him, their bodies grinding against each other as she rolled her head to the other side.

"I want you," she murmured, almost involuntarily. Michael's presence tended to do that to her. Of course, he had no way of knowing that she meant a lot more than sex. She'd be lying if she said that she didn't want him for real. She didn't want to think about how incapable he was of taking this as seriously as she did.

A rough groan left the depths of his throat. "That's a very good thing, Charlie. I'm not sure I could live through it if you didn't."

If only that was true. She pushed aside the thought as he unzipped her dress. The garment slid down her arms and slumped to the floor. She turned and reached for his arm to brace herself as she stepped out of the gown. She expected him to pull her into his arms as soon as she straightened, but he actually stepped back. His eyes were heavy with desire as they raked over the length of her body. Michael had a very big weakness for sexy lingerie. From the look on his face, the way his mouth went slack, her black bustier and panties, made of the finest French lace, had been a very smart choice for this evening.

"You're so sexy. I don't want to take my eyes off you." He yanked at his tie and threw it on the floor as if he couldn't stand the thing.

"Then don't. Don't take your eyes off me." She floated next to him and pushed his coat from his shoulders, then untucked his shirt while he unsubtly peered down into her cleavage.

"Your breasts look incredible in that."

She was about to say that he had no idea, but she'd let him figure that out for himself. Pregnancy had rounded out her endowments nicely. The truth was that she was far less concerned with what was under *her* clothes than what was under *his*. It had been months since she'd seen Michael naked and she didn't want to waste another minute. Her fingers flew through the buttons of his shirt, no small task when he wouldn't stop kissing her. How dumb she'd been that day when they'd walked the dogs and she'd told him to stop kissing her. Whatever heartache was waiting on the other side of Michael Kelly's kiss was surely worth it.

The moonlight in the living room made the sight of his bare chest that much more beguiling. Shadows of blue, black and gold hit every carved ridge of his torso and abs. She pressed her palms against his chest and smoothed her hands over his muscles, which seemed to twitch beneath her touch. She drew in a deep breath and went for his belt. The clatter of metal played nicely against the moan that came from his lips as he kissed his way down her neck. With a pop and a zip, she let his pants drop to the floor. Then she made quick work of his boxer briefs.

It was her turn to torture him, as she stepped away and admired him in the light.

"Get over here," he said.

She shook her head. "I'm enjoying the view." As heavenly as it was to touch him, looking at him was a close second. He was as solid as a man could be, a looming tower of muscle. At the moment, some parts of him were more solid than usual. She couldn't wait to have him in her hand. She couldn't wait to have him inside her.

"No more looking, Charlie. Get over here. I need you to touch me."

She took her time breaching the few feet between them. She'd spent too many nights crying over Michael. If she was going to make a mistake and sleep with him, she wanted to at least feel in charge. She pressed her chest against his, letting him get another eyeful, as she reached down and wrapped her hands around his steely length. "Like this?"

"Yes." He cleared his throat and his chin dropped. She studied his face as his eyelids fluttered shut for a moment and he seemed to grapple with the firm strokes she was taking with her hand.

He cupped the sides of her face and kissed her, fast and loose. Their tongues wound in a dizzying spiral and she didn't let go of him. She caressed softer, loosening her fingers and letting the weight of his erection rest against her palm. He buried his hands in her hair, making a huge mess of it. She couldn't have cared less.

"I have to have you." Michael dropped their kiss and reached down to shimmy her panties past her hips.

Charlotte planted her hands on his shoulders. "We need a condom." No, pregnancy was not a concern, but she had no idea who'd he been with since they'd broken up.

"Two secs. Don't move." He hustled into his room and Charlotte followed orders, staying put. He was back in seconds flat.

"All better?" she asked.

"All better. Now, where were we?" He lifted her up, his fingers sinking into the soft flesh of her bottom as he thumped her back against the wall next to the living room window.

He positioned himself at her entrance and drove inside, strong and forceful. Charlotte wrapped her legs around his waist as her body came to terms with how completely he filled her. Her hands clasped his neck, urging his mouth down to hers. Having him inside her while his lips were on hers was the full-on Michael Kelly package—hot and wet.

He had one hand at the small of her back, but the other hand went to the bustier she was still wearing. He expertly popped open the top three clips and peeled back the lace to reveal her breasts. He pulled her body closer and dropped his head, his lips taking in the taut skin of her nipple. He looped his tongue and she felt her body tighten beneath that touch. It was enough to make the pressure and heat between her legs double.

He again pulled her close and lifted her back from against the wall. He turned and sat on the sofa, Charlotte straddling his lap. Now that he no longer had to hold her, he took care of the final hooks on her garment, and the lace fell to the floor behind her. He took both breasts in his hands and cupped them, rubbing his thumbs back and forth across her nipples, building heat and pressure inside her. He was so strong and nimble, he had no problem lifting her off the couch with his hips, taking strokes that went deeper and deeper. Charlotte thought her eyes might cross from the pleasure, it was so immense.

"Are you close, darling?" His voice was rough.

She nodded, closing her eyes, concentrating on how good and primal this felt. She'd needed this. Maybe this would get Michael out of her system. Hopefully, it wouldn't make things worse. Hopefully, it wouldn't deepen her attachment to him.

He slipped his thumb against her apex and began rotating in small circles, using an ideal amount of pressure. Michael knew she needed some help, and he wasn't afraid to give it. He was definitely the kind of man who wanted her to come first, sometimes more than once. It was one of his many, many selling points. She ground her body against his hand—it felt so good, the insides of her body winding tighter, her hips feeling fitful and restless. She was so close to the edge she could feel herself unraveling, and with a jolt, she gave way. She tossed her head back and called out, placing her hands on his thighs behind her. He followed while the waves of pleasure were still rocketing through her, unleashing himself into her in strong pulses. It was as hot as she could've imagined. She collapsed forward, burrowing her head in his neck. He wrapped his arms around her waist and pulled her close, smoothing back her hair and kissing her cheek.

She'd thought making love with Michael might help get him out of her system, but after their red-hot tryst, she knew it would take at least a few more tries.

Eight

In the soft light of morning, Charlotte's eyes popped open, and she lay frozen in Michael's bed. *What did I do?* The question to herself was quickly answered by a lightning-fast barrage of images from last night—their exodus from the wedding, the kiss in the elevator, the invitation to his apartment, the moment when clothes came off and, of course, the wall.

She clutched the sheets to her chest, careful not to move or breathe too loud while she tried to sort through this in her brain. What did this mean? Did Michael want her back? She'd been very clear on their walk that there could be nothing physical between them when they were on such different pages. Had he changed his mind? Had a few minutes of Gabe Underwood–induced jealousy been enough?

If Michael did want more, it could be the answer to everything she'd spent months worrying about. Single parenthood would no longer have to be the biggest challenge to come. She could switch to regular parenthood, which would be its own feat, but at least she'd have someone to hand off the baby to in the middle of the night if things got particularly hairy. It could be amazing if Michael wanted to pick things up again, but there was only one problem. Charlotte's life did not magically work out that way.

Then there was the not-small matter of what she wanted, a priority she was still learning to put first. Did she even want to get back together with Michael? Would things be any better the second time around? Would he appreciate her? Would he ever love her? There were no guarantees. Her old inclination was to search for meaning in his words, like a woman reading tea leaves. She was such a sucker for a well-delivered line, especially when it came from a mouth as gorgeous as Michael's. Last night's, out on the dance floor, had been a doozy. *I made a mistake when I let you go.* But no. She needed to stop judging a man first by his words and second by his actions. Fran had spent a good chunk of time drilling this into her head: *It's actions first, words second, Charlotte. Not the other way around.*

Judging Michael by his actions was Job One this

We'd like to send you two free books like the one you are enjoying now, absolutely free!

Dear Reader,

You see the **Jack of Hearts sticker** on the front of this card? Simply paste that sticker in the box on the Free Merchandise Voucher to the right. Return the Voucher today... and we'll send you Free Merchandise worth over $20 retail!

Thanks again for reading one of our novels—and enjoy your Free Merchandise with our compliments!

Pam Powers

Pam Powers

REMEMBER: Your Free Merchandise, consisting of **2 Free Books and 2 Free Gifts**, is worth over $20 retail! No purchase is necessary, so please send for your Free Merchandise today.

Get TWO FREE GIFTS!
We'll also send you 2 wonderful FREE GIFTS (worth about $10 retail), in addition to your 2 Free books!

Visit us at:
www.ReaderService.com

Books received may not be as shown.

YOUR FREE MERCHANDISE INCLUDES...

2 FREE Books **AND** 2 FREE Mystery Gifts

FREE MERCHANDISE VOUCHER

2 FREE
BOOKS
and
2 FREE
GIFTS

Please send my Free Merchandise, consisting of
2 Free Books and **2 Free Mystery Gifts**.
I understand that I am under no obligation to buy
anything, as explained on the back of this card.

225/326 HDL GMVQ

Please Print

FIRST NAME

LAST NAME

ADDRESS

APT.# CITY

STATE/PROV. ZIP/POSTAL CODE

NO PURCHASE NECESSARY!

HD-N17-FMFC17

READER SERVICE—Here's how it works:

morning. Would he offer to bring her coffee? That would be a point in her mental "yay" column. Be sweet? Want to make love again? Yay and yay. As exciting as the prospect was of things finally moving in the right direction, she needed to temper her expectations. And get on with it already. She needed to wake him up.

Prepared to press a gentle morning kiss to Michael's cheek, she carefully and quietly rolled over.

To an empty bed.

She tore back the covers as if all six feet and many more inches of him could possibly be hiding under there somewhere. "Michael?" she called, sitting up in bed. No answer. She patted down the mattress for a hint of residual body heat, but the sheets were as cold as if no one had slept there at all. She climbed out from under the duvet and hustled over to his dresser, pulling out a soft, worn T-shirt of his and threading it over her head. It lightly skimmed her legs, the hem coming down to the middle of her thighs. "Michael? Are you up?" She used her voice a little more forcefully now, but there was still no reply.

Maybe he went out to get pastries and coffee. The passion-fruit Danish from the bakery a few blocks away. Yes, that was it. That had to be it. That was a nice and thoughtful thing to do. She walked into his bathroom, peed and washed her hands, then ventured out into the apartment, hoping to find a note. Her search for evidence of a sweet, early morning scone run turned up nothing more than a neat stack of her clothes from yesterday on the end of his couch. He'd spent enough time milling around the apartment this morning to do that? What else had he done? And where had he gone? Her heart began to thump anxiously. Her heart knew what was up, but her brain was still computing.

Abby was also gone. Aha! He'd probably taken her downstairs for a few minutes. That didn't completely warrant a note, right? Maybe a text was in order. She pulled her cell out of her handbag.

Hey. Where are you?

As hard as she stared at her phone, no answer came. With every passing tick of the clock, and every lap she took in his living room, Charlotte realized more and more that she was making excuses for Michael. If the situation had been reversed, she would've left a note. She wouldn't have slept with someone and dared to leave her apartment for more than two seconds without letting the other person know what she was doing. She would have replied to a text, no matter the circumstances. This was classic Michael and the problem with classic Michael was that he knew how to please her in bed, but everywhere and everything else was sorely lacking.

She needed to put an end to her own idiocy. She needed to stop acting like Charlotte, and start acting like Michael—cold and calculating, taking what he wanted and leaving everyone else to fend for themselves. She scooped up her clothes from the wedding and decided it wasn't even worth it to change. She and Michael were still the only residents of their floor and it was very early Sunday morning, only a few minutes after seven. She'd be fine to bolt down the hall to the safety of her apartment.

She opened the door and first made sure the coast was clear. She doubted she'd run into a member of the hotel staff, but she wanted to be sure. Holding her head high, she marched down the hall, but she began to shrink with every step. This walk of shame reminded her too much of the night she and Michael broke up. It left her with the same empty feeling, but now it was more pronounced, leaving her feeling even more hollow. That time, she hadn't been aware that she was pregnant with Michael's child.

Just as she passed the elevators, she heard it ding. Half-naked, her survival instinct kicked in and she ran to her end of the hall, but she stopped as soon as she rounded the corner and was out of sight. She poked her head out to see Michael, Abby and a woman step out into the hall.

"Do you mind waiting here for a moment?" he asked the woman. "I just need to put my dog in my apartment, then I can give you a tour of some of the available units."

"Of course. I'll wait." The woman was statuesque

and raven-haired, and although there was no hint of romance between her and Michael, the fact that she was beautiful irked Charlotte.

A showing? He's doing a showing? He's impossible. Charlotte had seen enough. She keyed into her apartment and closed the door behind her, collapsing against it. She was still ruminating over what was going on when Thor yelped from the confines of his crate. She let him loose, thankful she'd thought enough to text Fran last night and ask her to take him out. He yipped and vied for her attention, so Charlotte invited him up onto the couch and endured countless licks and doggy kisses.

"Abby's dad is mean," Charlotte said to Thor. "He's a real jerk."

Thor stopped licking for an instant and cocked his head, making his ears flop.

"I don't think you should run down there anymore. Whatever it is that you think you have going on with Abby probably isn't going to happen anyway, buddy. She's too much like Michael. Too much on her own plan." The more she thought about this, the angrier she got. He'd had an appointment for a showing? That was why he hadn't left her a note. He hadn't wanted her to know what he was doing. That was Michael, though—always selling and always competing. Why she should fault a duck for looking and acting like a duck was beyond her.

Her phone beeped with a text. She anxiously dug

it out of her evening bag while anger wedged itself in
her thoughts. She was ready to give Michael a piece
of her mind…only to see that the text was from Noah.

Meet you in the lobby in fifteen?

Oh, crap. She'd completely forgotten that the family
was meeting for breakfast with Sawyer and Kendall
before they left for their honeymoon. With Christmas almost here, they were only going away for a few
days, down to Miami. They had a longer trip planned
for January. Sawyer had been insistent that the three
siblings were going to spend more time together now
that he had a child on the way. Things were not going
to be splintered just because their father seemed to
want things that way. Charlotte agreed, especially
with her surprise bun-in-the-oven.

Make it thirty? There was no way she'd be ready
to go in fifteen minutes.

Plus, she had a text of her own to send. Another
one, to Michael. Thanks for letting me know where
you were this morning. So nice to wake up to an
empty bed. Michael was fluent in sarcasm. It was
one of the best ways to get to him.

Noah replied, Moving a little slow this morning?

Charlotte couldn't help but think that a hangover
would be better than the bitter sting of reality Michael had handed her this morning. Just primping.
You know me.

Okay. I'll let everyone know you'll be late.

Where did you go? This time, the text was from Michael.

She wrestled with how to reply—she had nothing in the way of a snappy comeback, although if she could come up with one, she'd find a way to include Gabe in it. That would get under his skin. But with only a half hour to shower and get downstairs for breakfast, she decided it was better to let Michael stew in his own juices.

In world-record time, Charlotte showered, put on her makeup, dressed, zipped Thor downstairs for a pee break, begged a bellboy to return the dog to her apartment and was in the hotel restaurant, headed to the very back, where her family—Noah, Aunt Fran, Sawyer and Kendall—was nearly finished splitting one of the Grand Legacy's world-famous cinnamon rolls.

"So sorry I'm late," Charlotte said, taking hugs from her brothers, who had both gotten up from the table. Consummate gentlemen.

Sawyer waved it off. "We're used to it by now."

Charlotte took her place in between her oldest brother and Fran, then ordered a cup of herbal tea and asked the waitress if she could bring another cinnamon roll. She'd missed out on too much of that yummy action. Kendall grasped Sawyer's arm and rested her head on his shoulder. The one thing Char-

lotte had noticed yesterday at the wedding, which was
even more noticeable now, was just how comfortable
they were with each other. It was like they'd known
each other their whole lives. Maybe that was the yard-
stick for a good relationship—when you find someone and you effortlessly fit together. It doesn't have
to mean it's perfect. Every couple argues. But some
people are simply meant for each other. Sawyer and
Kendall seemed to be that couple.

Charlotte couldn't help but be at least a little bit
jealous. It would've been nice if she could've gotten
pregnant by the one man on the planet, wherever he
might be, who was right for her. But at this point,
lots of things would be nice, and as Fran had said a
million times, dwelling on the past was going to get
her nowhere.

"Where'd you get off to last night, Charlotte?"
Noah asked. "We missed you at the end of the reception."

Fran cast Charlotte a sly look and took a sip of
her coffee.

Oh, yeah. That. "I was tired. I didn't want to bring
down the whole party by falling asleep at the table."

"You didn't seem tired. You danced for quite a
while with Michael Kelly." The tone in Sawyer's
voice was unmistakable, and Charlotte couldn't help
but recall the first time this subject had come up between the two of them.

"He was rambling on about real estate. He can talk

about it forever. I swear the man just likes to hear his own voice. I'd tell him to shut up, but sometimes he actually shares valuable information."

"You two are cute together," Kendall added. "He's really quite handsome."

"We've been married fewer than twenty-four hours and you're already scouting out other guys?" Sawyer asked, cocking an eyebrow at Kendall.

She swatted his arm. "Shush. It's the truth. And I was talking about him in the context of your sister, not me. I'm sure Charlotte would love to meet a nice guy."

Charlotte nearly sputtered a mouthful of tea across the table. All she could do was nod and smile. Of course she wanted to meet a nice guy. She just wasn't sure where exactly a girl went about finding one.

A grin crossed Fran's face. "Speak of the devil. Look who's on his way over here right now." She gave Charlotte a little kick under the table for good measure.

Everyone at the table looked up, and sure enough, here came Michael. He was dressed in jeans and a black sweater, looking far more handsome than was fair. "I'm so sorry to interrupt your family breakfast. I was hoping to steal a moment with Charlotte."

"Can this wait until later?" she answered, looking up at him, hoping the tension in her face could convey how much she did not want to speak to him right now.

"It'll only be a minute. You haven't been answering my text messages."

Sawyer cleared his throat and that sent Charlotte into a panic. She didn't need to give her brother any more material to form an opinion of what may or may not be going on between herself and Michael. "Excuse me, everyone. I'll just be a second."

Michael blazed a trail through the restaurant and Charlotte followed. Whether she was mad at him or not had no bearing on the fact that he looked better than amazing in a pair of jeans. "What happened this morning? I was gone for twenty minutes and you disappeared. Did you not enjoy yourself last night?"

Charlotte's shoulders dropped in frustration. "I don't know how long you were gone, but I'm pretty sure it was more than twenty minutes. Regardless, I woke up, you were gone, there was no note and no explanation, but you sure took the time to fold my clothes. I even sent you a text and you didn't answer. It just started to feel an awful lot like a repeat of the old Charlotte and Michael show. I hate that show, Michael. Just so you know."

He frowned. "I didn't see the text until right before I sent one to you, which you didn't bother to answer, either. I figured I should let you sleep. I never imagined you would wake up so early."

"I always get up early, Michael. Do you really not remember that about me?"

He scratched his temple. "Yeah, I guess I remember that. I was mostly just thinking about how tired you seemed last night."

"Sex against a wall will do that to a person," she snapped. "And you had a showing this morning? Or were you trying to hide that from me?"

The look that crossed his face was pure annoyance. "I don't hide anything, ever. I took Abby for a walk, the woman I ended up showing the apartment to was in the lobby. She wanted to pet Abby, we started to talk and the next thing I knew I'd sold another unit."

Of course he'd sold another unit. How silly of her to think anything less could've happened. How these things just fell into his lap was beyond her. "I'm glad you've had such a productive morning. Look, last night was really fun, but you and I have a terrible time getting on the same page, so I think it's best if we just go back to the part with no kissing or touching."

"I thought we were spectacularly on the same page last night."

He was not kidding about that. They were. But sex wasn't enough to make her happy, just temporarily giddy. "That part is fine. It's everything else that's messed up. This morning has been the perfect illustration of that."

"I'm sorry I didn't leave a note."

"It's not an indictment, Michael. So you didn't leave a note. It's not about the note. It's about our complete incompatibility. I obviously need more than you're equipped to give, which is exactly why we broke up in the first place." She patted him on the shoulder. "Now, I need to go spend time with my family. I'll see you around, okay?"

"Around? What does that even mean?"

"The hall? The elevator? The lobby? Anywhere else and we just seem to get into trouble."

Nine

Judging by the view, being a professional woman really suited Charlotte. Michael watched as she approached him at the elevators—she was teetering on heels that made her legs far too appealing. Her skirt was full and swishy, her blouse crisp and fitted. Her blond hair was up in a twist, or was it a bun? Michael wasn't sure what it was called. He only knew that it was sexy as hell.

"Morning," she said, standing straight and looking only at the elevators.

"Morning, yourself." He was still trying to sort out what had happened at the wedding, and after it.

The elevator doors slid open and he gestured for

her to go first. He had Abby with him, and he firmly believed in being a gentleman. They stood inside, shoulders a polite distance apart, neither making eye contact.

"Busy morning?" he asked.

"I have a showing at ten. Eighteen B."

"No way. I'm showing Eighteen C at ten as well. On my way down to meet the client now."

"You're taking Abby?"

"He's a huge dog-lover. I figured she could help seal the deal."

She glanced at him for a second and nodded. "Nice. This was a referral from Gabe Underwood. The Taylors. John, Jane and their little boy. I'm meeting Gabe and them downstairs in a minute."

Ugh. And I thought today was going to be a good day. "So you got some business out of Gabe at the wedding?"

She twisted her lips and shot him a look. He hadn't meant for it to come out as a suggestive comment. "I did."

A big part of him wanted to just let this go, but he couldn't. "I hate that we've gone back to our old dynamic. It was more fun when we only hated each other a little."

"I don't hate you, Michael. I'm simply trying to protect my own feelings and concentrate on my career. If anyone should be able to appreciate that, it should be you. It's exactly what I told you. Nothing has changed." The elevator slowly pulled to a stop, then dinged and the doors slid open. Out she marched without him.

Indeed, nothing had changed. Except Charlotte. She seemed different now, and it was becoming more pronounced every day. She was more confident. She stood up for herself. She put him in his place. He'd never had to live with any remorse over losing a girlfriend before, but he was definitely suffering from the effects with her. Watching her walk around the world as if she didn't need him at all was again making him wonder just how badly he'd messed up when he'd let her go. "Okay, then," he muttered to himself. He followed her into the lobby, but Charlotte took strides so long he couldn't keep up, which was saying a lot considering how much longer his legs were.

Michael greeted his client, Samuel Baker, an art dealer looking to move back to New York after a few years in Los Angeles. Michael had sold him his last New York apartment. "I hope you found the hotel with no problem."

"Yep. Yep. Is this the same dog you had the last time?"

Michael leaned down and scratched Abby behind the ears. "The same one. This is Abby."

"Hello, beautiful," Mr. Baker said, showing her affection.

"Shall we head upstairs?" Michael couldn't stand another minute in the same space with Gabe Underwood. He was across the lobby, laughing like an idiot at Charlotte's jokes. He was so flirtatious with her, it made Michael insane. Couldn't she see that he was just sucking up to her as a means of getting more business from Sawyer and Noah? Or maybe she didn't care. Maybe she only wanted to get another buyer out of him.

Michael and Mr. Baker took the elevator, but Samuel was taking the hall at a pretty slow pace once they arrived on the eighteenth floor. It wasn't long before Gabe and Charlotte caught up to them, along with Gabe's clients, the Taylors and their son, who was toddling down the hall.

"Doggie!" the little boy exclaimed.

Mrs. Taylor tugged him along. "Yes. A doggie."

Michael opened up Eighteen C and went to work. Mr. Baker loved the layout of the living room and the views, which was all fantastic news, but Michael was again having a hard time focusing when he could hear Charlotte laughing from next door.

"Are the walls really that thin?" Mr. Baker asked.

Apparently. "Oh, it won't be that bad when there's furniture in both units and artwork on the walls. Plus, I know the agent next door and she's especially giggly. Don't worry. She won't actually be living there."

Mr. Baker nodded. He seemed convinced enough by the explanation. "Is that the blonde?"

"That's the one."

"She's a cutie. I mean, I know I'm not supposed to make comments like that, but she is."

"You're not wrong, Mr. Baker. You're not wrong at all. Now let me show you the master suite."

The rest of the showing went smoothly. Michael hardly had to sell at all, and that meant he was done well before Charlotte and Gabe were showing any sign of slowing down next door. Part of him wanted to hang around and find out what was happening, and another part of him knew he needed to get a life, get over Charlotte and get back to the office. He closed the door on what would soon be Mr. Baker's apartment and locked up. He was about to press the button to call the elevator when he heard a screeching yelp. He turned and the Taylors' little boy was headed straight for him.

"No!" the child yelled. "No new house."

Michael was terrible with kids, but somewhere inside he must have some protective instinct because he crouched down and spread his arms wide to keep the boy from running right past him. "What's up, little man?"

The kid collided with Michael's arms. His cheeks were puffy and red, his brown eyes wide with shock. Then he saw Abby. "Doggie!"

Abby had a different skill set than Michael when it came to children. She loved them and had the perfect easygoing attitude to go along with it. She dutifully let the boy pet her, sitting still and putting up with some rough handling. "Gentle." Michael demonstrated the proper petting technique.

Mrs. Taylor tore out into the hall. "I'm so sorry." She took the little boy's hand and turned to Charlotte, who had come out to see what was wrong. "This is the third place we've looked at today and I think he's had enough. My husband and I really think this is the place for us, but maybe we should come back on another day when out little guy isn't so tired."

Charlotte nodded, but you could see the disappointment on her face. "Of course. Whatever you think is best."

"I'm happy to hang out here with him in the hall if you guys need to finish up." Michael wasn't sure what had come over him. He liked Charlotte, he cared about her and wanted to see her succeed, but he wasn't the guy who typically tried to save the day. He had a mountain of work to do. And yet, he couldn't walk away when he knew that one tiny favor might do Charlotte some good.

Mrs. Taylor turned back to Michael with a questioning look. "Are you sure?"

"Yeah. He loves the dog. She clearly loves him. We'll just play for a few minutes." Michael sat down on the floor and leaned back against the wall, still holding on to Abby's leash and keeping a close eye on the little boy and the dog.

"That would be amazing. Thank you so much."

Mrs. Taylor turned to Charlotte and squealed. "That means we can buy a house today."

Charlotte looked right at Michael, her beautiful blue eyes pulling on him like they had their own gravitational force. "Thank you," she whispered. "I owe you one."

"I'll keep that in mind," he muttered to himself after she'd gone.

After about twenty minutes, the Taylors emerged from the apartment and retrieved their son.

"Thank you, again," the dad said.

"No problem," Michael replied, standing up and brushing his pants clean. He gave Abby a pat for her extrapatient behavior.

Gabe and Charlotte were next to appear as the Taylors took the elevator downstairs.

"She was amazing in there, Kelly," Gabe said. "I gotta tell you, she really knows her stuff, and she couldn't have been any more charming if she tried. My clients fell in love with Charlotte well before they fell in love with the unit. Which they just bought, I should mention."

Charlotte blushed and playfully knocked Gabe in the arm. "Stop. You're embarrassing me."

Michael had no doubt that when it came to charm, Charlotte could win lots of people over. Maybe that was part of the reason why he just couldn't seem to get over her—she was constantly amazing him and proving him wrong. He'd always contended that real estate was a business only for the truly brutal, but judging by the look on Charlotte's face, she was managing to do pretty well by simply being her normal lovely self.

Gabe consulted his watch. "Well, I have to scoot. The Taylors are waiting for me downstairs. You sure you don't want to join us for lunch? I'm sure the Taylors would love it."

Charlotte grinned wide. She was so full of pride she looked as though she was about to explode. Michael could remember what it was like when this was all new. Maybe he wasn't tough. Maybe he was just jaded. "I'm so sorry. It sounds wonderful, but I have two more showings this afternoon and some other work to do."

Gabe held up his hands in mock surrender. "I get it. You're busy. Not surprised. Just keep it up." He grasped her elbow and kissed her cheek. "Maybe you and I can have a meal on our own some time. Celebrate the sale, together?"

Michael was as uncomfortable as he'd ever been. He found his fingers coiling in his palm, like they were itching to unleash one well-placed punch.

"That's very sweet of you. I don't like to mix business and pleasure, but if you want to have dinner as colleagues, that would be quite nice."

The disappointment on Gabe's face was a nice reward. Michael felt like he could exhale. "Oh, sure. Of course." He didn't look at Michael at all. "I'd better head downstairs."

"Nice save," Michael said when Gabe was finally gone. "It's not easy to turn someone down for dinner."

"It wasn't a save. I have no interest in Gabe. He's a nice enough guy, but our relationship is about work and nothing else."

Michael had to temper the good feelings her statement brought about. She'd made the same argument about Michael, too. Just work. No pleasure.

"Headed down to your apartment?" he asked.

"Yeah. I need to call Noah and make a plan with him. He wants me to do a walk-through on a project he and Sawyer are thinking about taking on. They want my opinion."

"Residential?"

"Yeah. Downtown. I'm hoping this means good things for me." They made their way to the elevator. "Noah hinted that they might have another project for me to work on. At first I'd thought I only cared about the listings in the Grand Legacy, but now that we're getting down to the wire, I need to start thinking about what's next, you know?"

"Of course." He had to wonder what else or who else she saw in her future. Could he ever catch up to her and be comfortable with the idea of more than casual?

"Thank you again for helping with the Taylors' son."

"I was happy to help. It's funny, because I'm usually terrible with kids. But that little guy was pretty nice."

She shot him an indecipherable look and sighed. "Well, thank you."

"So. Another sale. How many more units does that leave for you?" he asked.

"Three. You?"

"I'm down to two."

This time, she didn't seem in any way defeated by the knowledge that he was ahead in their race. "It's close. I predict a photo finish."

They rode the elevator down to the fifteenth floor. Michael was overcome with a deep desire to kiss Charlotte. She'd always been irresistible, but right now, it went well beyond that. She seemed brighter, more beautiful, so full of life. Perhaps it was the shine of success. It looked good on her.

"Hey. I'm still hosting that cocktail party I told you about. The one on the twenty-third?"

"Ah. The family avoidance party?"

"And networking. Don't forget that. I'm having it downstairs in the cellar bar. Do you want to come? You didn't give me a definitive answer the first time."

"Is this a date? Because I'm not going as your date."

Wow. He really was in the same miserable boat as Gabe. "I'd like to be able to buy you a drink, if that's what you're asking. We could even ride the elevator together."

She thought long and hard. "Okay. Yes. I'd love it. Thank you. As long as this is about work and nothing else."

"It's nothing else. I promise."

Ten

Charlotte had to go to Michael's party. It would be stupid not to go. Downright foolish. There would be professional contacts to be made, better yet in the scope of a social gathering. Charlotte could rock a party like nobody's business. She was built for it. The trouble was the host. Michael was built for making her do stupid things.

Fresh out of the shower, hair up in a towel, she attempted to apply liquid eyeliner—no easy feat in itself—but her hand wouldn't stop trembling, leaving her with more of a fat wobbly smudge than a chic and seductive cat eye. It was all her dumb heart, nervous about tonight. It couldn't settle on the proper speed, so it was instead jumping up and down like an overcaffeinated rabbit, sending quakes and tremors through her arms and legs. She set down the tube of eyeliner on the bathroom counter and drew in a calming breath, looking at herself in the mirror. Hers was not the face of an in-control businesswoman. Frankly, all she could see was the same desperate teenage girl, her old self, clamoring for approval and love. *I have to get a grip.* She had to keep Michael at a professional distance tonight. He may have worked his way into her better graces by watching the Taylors' son, but tonight was about proving a point to herself. She had to know that she and Michael could coexist on an amicable, platonic level. The trouble was the tone of Michael's voice in the elevator when he'd reminded her of the party. Every time she'd ever heard him talk that way, they were either *in* bed or *on* their way there.

Her heart couldn't afford another trip into Michael's bed. With the baby on the way, she had to keep her lines drawn. She had no doubt that the instant she finally revealed the news to Michael, that's what he would do. *I have the distinct impression you want far more from this relationship than I am prepared to give.* Even now, the words, which were permanently etched in her memory, stung like a fresh slice through her heart. There was no mistaking just how damning those words were, especially for a woman in love. Talk about closing a door on their future—

Michael had slapped a padlock on it and promptly tossed the key.

Of course, he'd had to keep tempting her with his physique and sharp wit, with his smarts and the way he looked in a pair of jeans. He had no clue what was on the line. They weren't even on the same playing field anymore. He thought they were flirting. He thought they'd had a fun night of hot sex. She had to set him straight, but not until her half of the Grand Legacy units were sold. By then, she could tell her family. By then, she could tell Michael and they would no longer have work entanglements. She didn't want him to back down from their competition because she was pregnant with his baby. She wanted to win this, fair and square, if only to prove to herself once and for all that she could make it on her own.

But first, she had to find a dress she could still fit into. Rifling through her closet, she knew on a purely practical level which one it would be—the red one. The one she'd bought a year ago at a designer sample sale. It had been a size too big, which was reason enough to buy it, as there was nothing more fun than stepping out of the dressing room in a fancy designer showroom and hearing the sales woman declare, "Oh, my! It's much too big." Charlotte had been having a skinny day that day. Probably because she'd recently recovered from a stomach virus. Regardless, the dress had been a steal, and she'd brought it home, but she'd never worn it. Now that she was a good five pounds heavier, it was the perfect choice.

She slipped her way into it and took a gander in the full-length mirror in her bedroom. The dress was professional. No ruffles, no thigh-high slit or plunging neckline. But it was off-the-shoulders, and the simple silhouette left nothing to the imagination. Of course, Michael needn't search far in his memory to recall what Charlotte looked like naked, but the dress and the idea of him seeing her in it still made her nervous. She turned sideways in the mirror and smoothed her hand over the tiny pooch. That was a baby. Her baby. For now, if anyone asked, she'd simply say she'd hit the Christmas cookies and eggnog a bit early this year.

She glanced at the clock. It was already after eight. She believed in the notion of being fashionably late, but Michael was a stickler for punctuality. He wouldn't take kindly if she pushed things too far. She popped in a pair of sparkly earrings, stepped into the bathroom to smooth out the bad eyeliner job and then went into her closet to work her way into the only red shoes she owned—sky-high and strappy. A month from now, she probably wouldn't even be able to get her feet into these shoes and her center of gravity would be all kinds of wrong. She might as well milk tonight for all it was worth.

Charlotte arrived downstairs at the newly opened cellar bar by eight twenty. The room was absolutely buzzing with frenzied conversation, with cheerful holiday music as a softer counterpoint. Charlotte eased her way inside, scanning the crowd for Michael. This space was another of Sawyer's many triumphs in bringing the Grand Legacy to its former glory. The ceiling's soaring archways were clad in warm white mother-of-pearl tile, accented with narrow strips of black glass. The original wrought-iron chandeliers had been restored and were stunning when lit, tastefully decorated with fragrant swags of fresh pine garland and holly berries.

Off in the far corner, next to the bar, Michael was talking animatedly with another man of similar build and stature. Not many humans could claim such an impressive physical pedigree, and Charlotte was dying of curiosity to know who it was. She saw a few people she knew as she threaded a path for herself through the crowd. At least she'd have some people to talk to after she'd chatted with Michael. She didn't want to take too much of his time tonight, although part of that strategy was entirely her own self-interest. Every minute with him made her more confused.

"There he is," Charlotte said as she greeted Michael. "Our brave and fearless host."

She loved the way the utterly charming smile broke effortlessly across his face. He was enjoying himself. For a man with the world at his feet, he didn't seem to do that nearly enough. "Hello, Charlotte. It's good to see you." He put his arm around her and gave her a friendly squeeze. "Especially in that dress," he muttered into her ear. "Wow."

Charlotte was sure that people fifty feet away could feel the heat radiating from her face. Michael's compliments did that to her. "Thank you for the invitation. I appreciate it."

"Of course. I want you to meet my brother, Chris."

Charlotte felt as though a lightbulb was going off over her head. "Oh! You're Michael's brother. No wonder you're so freakishly tall and handsome."

Chris's grin and his laugh were almost exactly like Michael's. He shook Charlotte's hand, his fingers dwarfing hers. "It's nice to meet you. I've heard a lot about you."

Charlotte cast her sights up at Michael. "Whatever he said, it's a lie."

"Actually," Chris said, "he had nothing but good things to say."

Michael waved to someone in the crowd. "I think that's my cue to leave you two alone. Plus, I have a potential client on the line here. I want to get a drink or two in him and see if I stand any chance of finding him a place to live."

Chris leaned back against the bar. "He really did say a lot of nice things about you. Which is pretty surprising. He isn't always that forthcoming with his love life."

"But you know we're not involved anymore, right?"

Charlotte flagged the bartender and asked for her new usual—a club soda with lime.

Chris nodded. "He not only told me you broke up with him, I even got a phone call about it. Almost no women rank that highly with my brother. You should feel honored."

"Somehow it feels like more of a dubious distinction. Plus, it's not fair to say I broke up with him. It felt more like a set-up. He just made me do the dirty work."

"Interesting. I suppose every story has more than one side, doesn't it?"

"Yes, but my side is the right one." Charlotte smiled wide. She liked Chris. She could see that although the brothers were notoriously competitive, they were close. "So, what brings you to the big city? You live in Washington, DC, right?"

"I do. I've been coming at this time every year for a while now. I like to lend my brother the moral support, even if he insists he doesn't need it."

"Moral support for what? Christmas?"

"No. It's—" Chris stopped right in the middle of his sentence. His brows drew together in a look that Charlotte could only describe as dumbfounded. "Do you not know about this?"

The tone in Chris's voice sent shivers down Charlotte's spine. "I have absolutely no idea what you're talking about. Michael never talks about himself. I'm shocked I knew he had a brother in the first place. No offense, but he doesn't talk about your family much at all. It's mostly in the context of swimming and how much your childhood revolved around that."

Chris cast his gaze in Michael's direction. "I'm not really sure I should spill the beans. I mean, there has to be some reason he never told you. And I know it still bothers him. He and our father don't even speak anymore because of it."

Charlotte grasped Chris's forearm. "Okay. You're going to have to tell me something. I need to know that he didn't murder someone."

Chris shook his head and laughed quietly. "No. No murder. Just an engagement party that went horribly wrong and two parents who expect nothing but absolute perfection from their sons."

"I'm all ears."

As Chris told her the story and Charlotte peppered him with questions, it became abundantly clear that Michael, the guy with the bulletproof veneer, the guy who never loses or suffers, had done exactly that. When he'd retired from swimming, his parents were gravely disappointed. They wanted him to bring home more Olympic gold, but Michael wanted out. He'd been dating a senator's daughter, and his parents decided that was his salvation. They told him he had to propose. He did, even though he didn't love her. They'd thrown an extravagant engagement party, but Michael couldn't go through with it. He'd been bullied enough. Michael called it off. At the party.

In front of two hundred guests Michael hardly cared about, his father flew into a rage. He unleashed a tirade of Michael's faults, his failures and missteps. Michael couldn't take it anymore. His dad threw a punch and missed. Michael countered and his fist landed square on his dad's jaw. Everything after that spiraled down. There was no reconciliation. There was no forgiveness. Michael was an ungrateful disappointment and no longer welcome at home.

When Chris finished telling the story, he seemed so sad. There he was, stuck between his brother and his parents. And there was Michael, trying his hardest, and coming up short. Charlotte thought her childhood had been rough, but it was nothing compared to Michael's. And now that she had this giant chunk of new information, she had to wonder if she'd read Michael wrong all along.

Michael was keen to sign his potential new client, Alan Hayes, a hotshot tech whiz with very deep pockets, but he would've been lying if he'd said he wasn't distracted by Charlotte and Chris's conversation. It wasn't a bad diversion. Charlotte was jaw-dropping in that dress. He'd never thought of himself as a red-dress sort of guy. He was a bigger fan of black with a healthy dose of skin—a look Charlotte also carried off with no problem. But tonight? The red? Michael knew he was in trouble the minute she walked into the room.

He liked seeing Charlotte and Chris clearly enjoying their time together. Michael was an expert at keeping his family and friends separate. He'd raised it to an art. As close as they were, he'd even been hesitant to invite Chris to tonight's party. Normally when Chris came to town, they would go out to eat and catch a hockey or basketball game—anything that meant they could spend time together, but not get too mired in socializing. Nobody in Michael's professional life knew about his private past and he intended to keep it that way. It wasn't embarrassment. It was a topic he wanted dead and buried.

For that reason, he didn't want to leave Charlotte and Chris alone for too long. He and Chris were alike in many ways, but with one exception. Chris loved to talk, especially after he'd had a drink or two. "Hey, Alan," Michael said to his potential client. "Looks like you could use a refill on that Scotch. Why don't we go up to the bar? I'll introduce you to my brother and a good friend of mine."

Alan seemed game. "Yeah. Sure."

They made their way through the crowd. With every step closer to Charlotte and Chris, it became clear that their conversation was intense. Chris was talking a mile a minute. Charlotte's face showed everything from concern to shock. Michael hoped to hell his brother hadn't told her too much. He didn't want her thinking of him that way.

"Hey, you two. I hope those aren't long faces I'm seeing."

Charlotte looked up at him with eyes that could only be described as soft and forgiving. Considering the number of times she'd given him a look that was quite the opposite, it was more than a bit of a surprise.

"What? Us? No way," Charlotte replied, entirely too chipper. "Who's your friend?"

Michael introduced Alan, still trying to sort out what had gone on between Chris and Charlotte. Perhaps he was just being paranoid. Some old rules he made for himself might just need to be cast aside. He loved his brother and he cared deeply for Charlotte. They should be acquainted.

Alan immediately took to Charlotte. Although Michael had to wonder if the dress had something to do with it, the truth was that she was simply on a roll these days, charming and entertaining, comfortable in her own skin. She could've sold a brick to a drowning man.

"Hey, Michael," Alan began, "why should I hire you instead of Charlotte? If I want to move into a historic hotel, it seems like a no-brainer to buy from the woman whose family owns it."

Michael shrugged. "Yeah. You got me there. I have no good argument for that." He was surprised at himself. Normally he'd launch right into the long list of reasons he was a superior agent. If Gabe Underwood had been standing here, Michael would've gone for the jugular. But things were different with Charlotte. He'd figure out what to do about it, if anything, later.

Charlotte cast a quizzical look at him. "Excuse me, everyone. I think Michael must be very, very ill or quite possibly drunk." She grasped his elbow and held the back of her hand to his forehead. Their gazes connected and he endured the usual zap of electricity that came with it. He suspected that her effect on him might never go away. "Nope. No fever. I'm afraid we're going to have cut you off, mister. No more drinking until you're ready to go to the mat with me on who's the better real-estate agent."

All Michael could think was that he did want to go to the mat with Charlotte—if it meant rolling around on a horizontal surface. She was so damn sexy it boggled the mind. She wasn't second-guessing herself or trying to play off a compliment. She took everything as it came. Michael found her ability to roll with the punches irresistible.

"Personally, I think you two should work together," Chris said, pointing at Michael and Charlotte. "You could be the ultimate power couple. Nothing would stop you two."

"It didn't exactly work out the first time," Charlotte said.

Michael didn't know how to respond. There was a voice inside his head that kept telling him to try again with Charlotte. The voice was especially insistent tonight. The trouble was that if things didn't work out, untangling themselves as a couple would be far more complicated the second time. They lived in the same building now. She'd established herself in the same work circles. People loved to talk, especially about failed relationships.

"I think Charlotte and I might end up blowing up Manhattan if we worked together."

"Or you could end up being the biggest thing that's hit this town in a long time," his brother said.

Charlotte perched on a bar stool and crossed her lovely legs. When he looked at her for a reaction to the conversation, she was stirring her drink and stabbing ice cubes with the straw.

The party rolled on for at least another hour, but eventually the guest count began to dwindle. Alan excused himself, saying he had another party to attend. Chris was tired and headed upstairs to Michael's to crash. The bartender announced last call.

"I guess this is a wrap. Thanks for coming tonight." Michael swallowed hard, looking at Charlotte, trying to decide whether or not to listen to his inner voice. "You were the best part of the party. By far. I'm glad you had a chance to meet Chris. You two really hit it off."

Charlotte got up from her bar stool. He thought she was about to leave, but she instead took his hand. "We had a big talk. He told me a lot. Probably a lot of stuff that you didn't want me to know. I know about your parents. I know about your dad and the engagement. He told me everything."

So he'd been right. "I see." He braced for her reaction. Would she think he was less of a man? Would she think he was a monster for hitting his own father? He sought their strongest connection and looked at her. It took more than courage to gaze into Charlotte's eyes. It took reflection. Those big, beautiful blue eyes were like a mirror, showing Michael too much—everything he'd given up, everything he'd brushed aside, everything that had ever hurt him. It was sometimes torture to wade into these waters, but he had no choice now.

"I really wish you would've shared some of that with me, Michael. When we were together. It might have made things different between us."

He watched as her eyes misted and all he could think was that he was a horrible person. Could he ever come close to matching the good in Charlotte? He had pushed her away because he'd convinced himself that one traumatic event would determine the course of his life. He just couldn't own the failure, which was a defeat in itself.

"I know. You're right. It's just difficult for me to talk about. Still."

She stepped closer and held on to both of his arms. "I seriously feel like I'm seeing you in a whole new light."

"And?" He had to know how she saw him. He

didn't want to be weak, but somehow with her, he felt as though being vulnerable didn't have to be ugly. It didn't have to be a failing.

"It makes me want to take the hurt away."

Relief rushed through him. He'd worried that the truth would make her want to run away. "I'm not at all opposed to the idea."

She reached up and clasped her hands around his neck. Her fingers were soft, her touch warm. "I'm waiting for you to lean down so I can get to you. You're in a different atmosphere all the way up there."

He smiled and bowed his head, wrapping his arms around her waist. He placed the smallest kiss on her lips, but knew he would get lost in Charlotte if it lasted another second. He pulled back his head.

"That's it?" Charlotte jutted out her lower lip. He would've done anything to take a gentle nip.

"If we start something, I want to be alone with you. I don't want to stop. I don't want to have to think about anyone other than you."

Her cheeks plumped up when she smiled. "Oh. Okay. Good answer." She grabbed her evening bag from the bar. "Please tell me you don't have to settle up with the bar."

"No. They have my credit card. But I just remembered that my brother is upstairs in my apartment."

She smoothed her hand over his jacket lapel, then traced her finger down the front of his shirt. That one touch made every muscle in his body twitch. "We'll have to make do with my place."

"Will Thor even let me through the front door?"

"Thor loves you. He just doesn't know it yet."

Michael took Charlotte's hand, not caring who saw them like this. She might not have thought much of it, but it meant a lot to him. He was accustomed to being concerned with appearances at all times. His parents had trained him to think that way. He didn't care about impropriety anymore, or what people might say. He didn't care that everyone who worked in this hotel knew exactly who each of them was, or that they lived on the same floor upstairs. All he cared about right now was being with Charlotte.

They got the elevator to themselves and he didn't waste a minute. He took her into his arms and kissed her the way he'd wanted to downstairs—with intent, to send a message that he wanted her so badly he couldn't stand it. Scary or not, he wanted another chance. Her lips were impossibly soft and giving, her sweet smell the only air he cared to breathe.

They both jumped when the door dinged. He grabbed her hand again and they stole down the hall, this time to her apartment. Thor made this presence known with a bark as soon as they were inside, but Charlotte shushed the dog and Michael ignored him. Her hands were all over Michael as they kissed while practically stumbling through the foyer. They bumped into the wall, Charlotte with her back to it.

She groaned her approval and dug her fingernails into his biceps, tugging him closer as he deepened the kiss, but that wasn't what he wanted.

"No wall this time. I want to make love to you."

She took his hand and they hurried to her bedroom. Charlotte kicked off her shoes and pulled Michael over to the bed, shuffling backward as she went. She climbed up onto the mattress and unbuttoned his shirt, rocking from side to side on her knees. He loved her enthusiasm. She blew her hair from her face and yanked his shirt from the waist of his dress pants. He could hardly keep up with her and he wasn't sure he wanted to. She grabbed his shoulders and pulled him into a kiss, this one more frenzied than the one in the hall. With her full body weight, she flopped back on the bed, tugging him down on top of her. She slipped her leg between his, rocking back and forth, the firm pressure of her body making the blood rush to the center of his belly and due south. Their kiss was messy and perfect, fueled, he suspected, by what was new between them—his willingness to let down his guard. They were both so inspired it was like they might never stop kissing. He wasn't sure he'd ever been so hard—not even the time they did it against the wall.

Michael rolled onto his back, taking Charlotte with him. She straddled his waist, her dress hitching up her legs until it was around her hips. He sat up, but it took every ounce of strength he had in his abs to sit like that and unzip the back of her dress. He eased back down as Charlotte smiled at him and tossed her hair to one side. She was a vision he could've soaked up forever. So sexy. So sweet. He'd never met another woman like her. Did he love her? He was starting to think he might. That would've been unthinkable six months ago, but Charlotte had worn him down, even when she'd been trying to push him away.

She crossed her arms and lifted the hem of her dress, dragging the garment up the length of her body and revealing her creamy skin to him. In matching red lace panties and a strapless bra, she could be the subject of countless fantasies, and yet here she was, with him. He'd never felt so lucky in his life. "You're so beautiful, Charlotte. Why did I ever let you go?"

"I believe we've already had that discussion, but thank you. You're pretty damn handsome, but you already know that."

The grin on his face right now had to be regrettably goofy. He didn't care. She scooted back and to the side, then went to work on his pants and boxers, determinedly pulling them down past his hips and flinging them onto the floor. Now that they were gone, she again bracketed his legs with hers, but she'd stationed herself lower, with their feet touching. Her hands traveled up his thighs while a mischievous smile played on her lips. He knew exactly where she was headed and his stomach clenched in anticipation. His breath stalled in his chest. She dug in deeper with the heels of her hands as she reached his pelvis, firm pressure on either side of his erection, making it impossible to think straight, or see straight, either. She was taking her sweet time, torturing him with every second of delay, but it made the moment when she finally gave in so much better. She shimmied closer and her graceful fingers wrapped around his length. He drew in a deep breath and sank into the sensation. She stroked hard with one hand, looking deeply into his eyes, a connection he had many times found too deep to endure. He loved the in-charge version of Charlotte. To her, and only her, was he happy to relinquish control.

A deep groan rumbled out of his throat when she took the strokes faster. If he wasn't careful, he was going to be way ahead of her. He reached around to her back and unhooked her bra, but the vision of her plump breasts and hard nipples only brought him closer to the edge. As good as her touch felt, he pulled her into his arms, flat against his torso, and wrapped her up in a kiss unlike any other. He rolled her to her back and laid on his side against her, admiring every inch of her beauty. His hand caressed her silky belly, soft and smooth, then he slid it inside the front of her panties and found her apex. She sharply sucked in a breath as he employed one finger to do his bidding, creating tiny circles and a good deal of hot friction. The tiny bundle was tight and hard, but everything around it was wet and warm. She was as ready as she'd ever been, and he was so ready to be inside her that it physically hurt to wait, but he loved watching the look on her face as she closed her eyes and gave in to the pleasure.

"We're going to need a condom," he muttered into her ear, his fingers keeping steady time.

She opened her eyes halfway. He didn't mind that his touch might be making it hard for her to think. "Bedside table drawer."

He hated to stop touching her, but this had to be done. "One sec."

"Hurry."

He did exactly that, tearing open the package and putting it on. "I'm back." He returned his hand to his previous charge, sliding his palm down her belly and starting in gentle circles.

A smile broke across her face and her eyes drifted shut. "Good."

Her breaths were coming shorter now and he could tell she was close. Considering everything Charlotte had done for him, he wanted to bring her to her peak more than once tonight. He quickened his pace and stifled a smile when her mouth softened to an O, she jerked her head back on the pillow, and several gasping moans left her lips. He didn't wait for her orgasm to wane—he pulled down her panties and urged her up on top of him. He cradled her hips as she lowered her body. He closed his eyes as ecstasy threatened to overtake every inch of his body. She was so warm, her body still pulsing, now tightening around him. They began to move together in a rhythm that felt right from the first pass. They fit together so well it was as if they'd been built for each other. He took his thrusts as slowly and carefully as he could, but the reality was the pleasure was so tightly wound in his belly, he didn't have enough time to think before white light flashed through his head and the release rocketed through his pelvis. Charlotte gasped and it seemed that she was coming again, her body grasping him tighter.

As the waves began to ebb and everything blissfully sank bank down to earth, Michael pulled Charlotte against his bare chest. He rolled to his side, carefully dotting her face and shoulder with slow, deliberate kisses. All stress was gone. As he felt his body about to give in to sleep, he snugged her closer, wanting to feel her warmth all night long. Only one thought crossed his mind—Charlotte was perfect, and he'd better not let her go again.

Eleven

With the sun shining through her bedroom window and Michael's naked body next to her under the covers, Charlotte was nothing if not optimistic. Was there anything better than waking up next to someone as smart, funny and good-looking as Michael? No. She was quite certain of that. She snuggled closer to him just to soak up his body heat. She loved the way he smelled in the morning, a faint mix of his cologne and musky man.

Michael jumped when she put her feet on his calves. "What are you made of? Ice?"

"I can't help it. I'm always cold. Especially this time of year. Just the thought of how cold it is outside makes me even more cold."

"That makes absolutely no sense." He turned onto his side, facing her, his head resting on the pillow. He had a crease across his cheek and his stubble was a little longer than it had been yesterday. She palmed the side of his face, and the feel of his unshaven jaw tickled her hand. She found herself getting lost in his eyes, so soulful and deep. Funny that she had once thought of them as cruel. That was before she knew about his past. She was sure there were more secrets to be unearthed, but it would take time to reveal everything swimming in Michael Kelly's head. Possibly years.

"What can I say? I defy all logic. You'll have to get used to it." She hadn't meant for any mention of them in the context of being a couple to slip so soon, but it had and there was no taking it back.

"I'm more than accustomed to ignoring sound judgment when it comes to you."

"Good. It's highly overrated anyway." His comment hung over her as a reminder of the words she needed to finally say to him, the potentially life-shattering news she had to share. She'd said to herself last night that she would tell him today. She had to stick to that. Sooner rather than later would be best. But she still feared his reaction. She'd just gotten him to the point where he'd sleep at her apartment, for God's sake. That was a first for the two of them. Announcing a baby on the way seemed like an impossible leap, but she could no longer exclude him from their shared reality. Not when she wanted more.

Thor barked insistently from the other room. The confession would have to wait a few more minutes. The discussion that would follow was not to be interrupted. "I'm going to run him downstairs for a potty break. I can be back in ten minutes."

Michael reined her in with his arms and kissed her forehead. "You are too beholden to that dog."

"You should talk. You wouldn't even still be here if your brother wasn't staying in your apartment."

"True. Tell you what, I'll put on coffee, you take the dog out, I'll be here when you get back."

"No note required."

"No note."

He smiled that Michael smile—effortless and sexy. So brilliant it took her breath away. All she could think looking at his face was that she loved him. But would he ever feel the same way? He seemed different this morning, much more relaxed. Everything he'd been hiding must have been weighing on him terribly. Maybe that could pave the way for happier days for them. She wanted to believe that could be the case.

She pecked him on the lips. "Perfect." She hopped out of bed, threw on some jeans and a sweater, her fluffiest hat and mittens and a big coat. She and Thor caught the elevator right away. He scurried across the lobby, bolted through the door and did his business on the very first tree. She walked him to the corner, but was too eager to get in from the cold and back to Michael, so they turned back. As they approached the hotel, she marveled at how beautiful the holiday decorations were in the daylight. Tomorrow was Christmas Day. She'd be spending time with her family and Michael had plans with his brother. They apparently always spent Christmas together since they'd been estranged from their parents. Would Michael want to change his plans when he knew what she had to tell him? She wanted to believe he would. Maybe he and Chris could come over to Sawyer's and they could start folding themselves into each other's lives.

When Thor and Charlotte got back to the fifteenth floor, the lovely aroma of coffee hit her nose immediately. Charlotte couldn't think of a more pleasant scenario than spending the rest of the morning with Michael and her dog. As long as everything went well with the pregnancy announcement. She reached for the doorknob, knowing her moment of reckoning was upon her. *Everything will be fine.*

She let Thor off his leash and walked into the kitchen. Michael wasn't there, but a full pot of coffee was. He had apparently not taken a cup for himself yet.

"Michael?"

"Yeah. In here." His voice came from the living room. It did not sound warm or inviting. Quite the opposite, actually.

When she rounded the corner, he was sitting on the couch, elbows resting on knees, staring at her bottle of prenatal vitamins. They had been on the counter in her bathroom. Right where anyone could see. He picked it up and turned his head to face her. "Please tell me these belong to someone else."

All the warmth drained from Charlotte's body. She couldn't lie. It was bad enough she'd kept the secret so long. "They're my vitamins. I'm pregnant."

Michael had sensed Charlotte might be hiding something, but there had always been an element of the unknown with her. He'd assumed it was something having to do with her family, or the hotel, or work.

But a baby? That hadn't entered his mind once. And to think he was going to tell Charlotte this morning that he loved her. That had to be put on hold indefinitely. She'd lied to him, about something so monumentally important he couldn't comprehend it.

"How did this happen? When did this happen?" The instant the words left his mouth, he felt both idiotic and betrayed. She'd been with someone else. After him. Of course she had. He'd practically dared her to break up with him and she'd made no secret of how angry she was about it.

"I'm about twelve weeks along. I found out I was pregnant about two weeks after we broke up."

He was normally the person who moved on quickly.

Charlotte was making him look like a wimp when it came to dating. "You found a new guy that quickly? Who is he? And why isn't he around?"

"Are you seriously this bad at math, Michael? Or did you just not pay attention in health class? I found out two weeks after we broke up. I was about three weeks along then…" Her voice trailed off and she closed her eyes.

Oh, God. He *was* dense. "I'm the guy?"

Her eyes shot open. It was like a blue laser beam. "Yes. You're the guy. I haven't been with anyone else."

Crushing, conflicting emotions smacked into him. Was this what it was like to be in shock? If so, it was awful. "Why didn't you call me? I should've been the first person you contacted when you found out."

"I know." She wrapped her arms around herself, and he waited for her to retreat. That had always been her reaction when things got tough or she was put on the spot—to run away. Instead, she planted her hands on her hips. "But here's why I didn't. You told me flat out that I wanted too much and you weren't going to give it to me. If being a good boyfriend wasn't on your agenda, I had zero reason to think fatherhood was going to go over well."

"Hey. I know I wasn't perfect, but you make it sound like I was the worst boyfriend ever."

"You really don't want me to go there, do you?" The blaze in her eyes was like a dragon breathing fire.

"I know. I know. We always stayed at my place and I should have paid more attention. We've been over this."

"Don't do that." She shook her head and pursed her lips. "Don't make it sound like I was being trivial or petty. Your job always came first. I was second. Or quite possibly third, after Abby."

"That's not fair. My career is important to me. And I've owned Abby for nine years. It's not like I'm going to neglect my dog."

"I understand all of that. It's still not fun to be constantly reminded of the pecking order and that you're at the bottom of it."

Michael was struggling to keep up, but rehashing the past wasn't going to help him figure out the more pressing problem—Charlotte was pregnant and she'd hidden it from him. "This is why you ran off to England, isn't it? I knew there was more to it than regrouping."

"Bravo, Mr. Detective." She rolled her eyes, making him exponentially more frustrated with her and this conversation. "You know, you make it sound like I ran away with the circus. It wasn't an impulsive thing. I needed support. Quite frankly, I needed my mom, but I don't have one, so I went to Fran and she welcomed me with open arms."

Michael had to admit he didn't like the idea of her going through this on her own, but that wasn't his fault. "You can't put that on me. If you'd just told me, I could've been your support system. I don't understand why you didn't extend me that courtesy. Isn't that just common sense?"

"Common sense is not saying anything because you already know the other half of the conversation. I was upset and confused. I wasn't about to have that talk with you. I couldn't do it. I was barely keeping myself together."

"How could you have possibly known what I would've said?" He got up from the couch and started pacing the room. Perhaps movement would help him calm down. He could feel his anger growing and he refused to let it consume him or cloud his thoughts, which were already murky enough. "I don't know what to say right now and if anyone should know what I would say, it's me."

"You need to stop being so defensive." Her voice was clear and decisive, but her eyes were doing their best to work their way into his psyche. She was being so unfair right now.

"Defensive? You hid a pregnancy from me. I don't know how else I'm supposed to act. I've had all of two minutes to wrap my head around this. And right now, I can't think past the fact that you and I have been spending time together over the last few weeks and you've had every opportunity to tell me you were pregnant and you didn't." He ran his hands through his hair. His forehead was starting to throb like he'd just hit it with a hammer. There was too much competing for attention in his head right now. *Me? A dad?*

She blew out a breath. "I know. And I'm sorry, but I had my reasons. I had to get our professional entanglements out of the way. And to be honest, I think I had to protect myself from you, Michael."

If anything stung, it was hearing those words. He hated the thought of her feeling that way. It was never his intention to hurt her when he told her he wasn't capable of giving everything she wanted. If anything, he was trying to protect her. He cared too much to let her believe that he could be her everything. Now the stakes were considerably higher. "I don't know how to respond to that. I would never hurt you."

"Whether you meant to or not, you did hurt me, and this conversation is just confirming my worst fears. I feel like you're showing me where this ends."

"So I've been saying exactly what you thought I would? Am I really that predictable? Or are you just some sort of soothsayer?"

She leaned against the wall and looked out the window. He could see the gears turning in her head. "Honestly? This is worse than I imagined."

"How could it possibly be worse?"

"Because we're arguing about why I kept the secret. You haven't said a single thing about what this is really about. I messed up. I made a huge mistake and I'm incredibly sorry. But you haven't even mentioned the baby. Not a single word."

A dark and dense silence fell on the room. He didn't want to admit that she was right. The beast inside him that refused to lose was determined to take the course where he won this argument and showed her just how much she was in the wrong. "What do you want me to say?"

"I want you to tell me how you feel. About the idea of becoming a dad."

That word was a dagger to his heart. It brought up every negative connotation he could imagine, but it wasn't as simple as hating his father. Michael's greatest successes in life and his fierce determination had come from his dad. Some of it was genetics. Everything else had come by sheer force. His dad had brutally pushed both his brother and him. Their dad accepted nothing less than perfection. His sons were going to be champions, and they would stand on that Olympic podium and raise their hands in victory after the gold medal had been placed around their necks. Their dad had pursued that at any cost—he'd thought nothing of withholding love and approval. If anything, he'd seemed to think it was precisely what they needed.

It took twenty-three years for Michael to learn

that his father's expectations extended well beyond the pool. He expected it in everything, and when Michael dared to put his own feelings first and break up with his fiancée the night of their engagement party, all hell had broken loose. Michael had failed in spectacular fashion, according to his father, and for that he deserved disdain and blame. The look of disgust on his father's face was permanently etched in Michael's memory. He'd witnessed it the few times he'd seen his dad since that night. After a lifetime of doing absolutely everything his dad had wanted, Michael learned that night that it would never be enough.

He sank down onto the couch again. "I never saw myself becoming a dad. I don't know that I'm capable of it." *I'm terrified I'm going to ruin some poor kid.* "When I told you that I wasn't prepared to give you what you wanted, it wasn't to hurt you, Charlie. It was to give you an out so I wouldn't end up hurting you."

He looked up to see the color drain from her face. "And now I'm going to have your baby. So what do we do now?"

"I need time. I need time and space to process all of this. It's a lot to heap on someone at one time."

Time? He needs time? Charlotte could hardly believe the words coming out of his mouth. And she didn't care to hear too many more of them today. "Sure. Take all the time you need." *Just don't expect me to care whenever you finally sort this out in your head.* She stalked into her room.

Michael followed. "Look, I have to go back to my place. My brother is over there all by himself. I should go be a good host."

A good host? They were never going to get on the same page. It was time to put things on her terms. She wasn't about to let Michael dictate everything. "Good. Goodbye. I'm finding it hard to look at you right now anyway." That last part was such a lie. Even when she was hopping mad at Michael, she still wanted to look at him.

"I don't really want to look at you, either, if we're being honest." He thrust his arm into his sleeve and began buttoning his shirt in a fury, his hair flopping to the side as he stared at her in anger. Charlotte paced in her room as a storm of sadness and regret churned in her head. She embraced her feelings, something for which she had quite a talent. If she was going to be miserable, might as well go all in. As much as she hated to see things end like this, at least the man was showing some damn emotion. For once, he wasn't being so closed off. He didn't even bother to put on his shoes. He simply scooped them up from the floor, grabbed his jacket from the back of the chair and stuffed his wallet back into his pants pocket. Without a word, he stormed out of the room and headed straight for the front door.

"So that's it, then?" She really didn't like hearing those words come out of her mouth. They bore too much resemblance to her final utterance the first time they broke up. At least she wasn't sobbing this time.

"For now, yes." He didn't even look at her. He opened the door, waltzed through it and let it slam behind him.

Charlotte stood there like a statue, staring at the back of her door. She loved this apartment—she loved the Grand Legacy—and she'd already had so many daydreams about what it would be like to bring the baby home here. But maybe it just wasn't meant to be. The thought of running into Michael in the lobby, the hall or, even worse, in an enclosed space like the elevator was horrible. Having to see his handsome face, breathe his beguiling smells and know that he hadn't wanted to be part of her future would be too much. How would she ever heal? She wouldn't. And that wasn't fair to her, nor was it fair to the baby.

She flung open her door and took off down the hall. Thank goodness no one had moved in to the other two units on their floor, the empty ones between them. Thor yipped behind her. The escape artist was again at work. She rounded the corner and Michael was a few steps from his door.

"Michael, wait."

"What now?" He whipped around, slicing into her with the frustration on his face.

"I can't live in the same building with you anymore. Not if this is the end between us."

He threw up his hands. "You not only think the absolute worst of me, you can't stand the sight of me, either?"

"It's too painful. I won't do it. Whoever sells their units first gets to stay. The other person has to move out." Even though it was a slightly insane idea, she was pleased that it came off sounding like something the ever-confident Michael would say.

He turned to her and shifted his armful of jacket and shoes to one side. "You don't want to do that. You love the Grand Legacy. If you make this deal, you're going to be the one who has to leave. I only have one more unit to sell and I already have a buyer on the hook. Another day or two and I win."

Of course he phrased it in that way. He thought of little else. "If that's what happens, that's what happens. I just want something resolved. For good."

"It's Christmas tomorrow. You want me to basically hand a pregnant woman an eviction notice at Christmas? I'm sure you'd love to be able to tell the world that I truly am an ass, but I won't do it."

"Stop assuming you'll win. I only have two units to sell. There's still a chance I could beat you. And no matter what happens, it was my idea. I fully own it." She felt good about dictating the rules of the game for once. She'd take any shred of control she could right now. This was progress.

He shook his head slowly and deliberately—classic dismissive Michael. "Whatever you want, Charlotte. But I still want you to at least give me some time to think. Don't go calling Chad from Hunks with Trucks."

"I'm not making any promises. I'm not going to sit around and wait forever." She patted her leg three times and Thor rushed to her side. She walked down the hall, trying her damnedest to muster an air of victory, waiting for her sense of accomplishment to kick in. As she opened the door to her apartment and Thor sidled past her inside, she realized that there was no way to win in this impossible situation. Either Michael loved her and wanted to be father to their child, or he didn't. He didn't know. He needed time. It might be cold or heartless, but something deep inside her said that wasn't good enough.

For Charlotte, love wasn't a question. It was an answer. She couldn't remember a time when she hadn't felt like that. It was her strongest need, a thirst that wouldn't go away, and she'd been working so hard to get past that, to get to a point where she didn't need so much of it. But when she thought about living her life being the sort of person who didn't need it so desperately, the future narrowed to a dark and unhappy point. She refused to accept that. She wouldn't live

like that. It was okay to be who she was. It was okay
that she would have love and she would give it. Every
day, just as she'd always wanted. That love would be
for her baby, and she would give it until her last dying
gasp. Everything that had been bottled up inside her
would finally come out, and she wouldn't stop until
it was spent and gone.

And somewhere else in this city would be Michael,
walking around with a chunk of her heart, completely
oblivious to everything he had missed.

Twelve

Michael woke up at seven thirty on Christmas morning, feeling more than a little hungover. He and Chris had stayed up late, playing cards and drinking. Not smart, but Michael had been nursing his wounds. He scrounged around in the covers until he found his phone, which was tucked under the pillow on the other side of the bed. He dared to look at it—no response to his many texts to Charlotte last night.

Can we talk? The first one had gone unanswered for an hour before he sent his follow-up.

You there? I'd like to talk about this. He'd sat on that message for two hours. Then he'd gone down to her apartment and knocked on the door. She never answered. So he went home and made another plea.

You have every right to be mad, but please just answer me. She hadn't had anything to say to that one, either. Charlotte always had her phone on, and she always had it with her. The only time she ever failed to respond was when she was mad. She'd done it the other day, when he hadn't left a note. For now, he was fairly certain he had his answer. *Go away, Michael.*

He rolled out of bed and Abby followed him into the kitchen. He filled her food bowl and started the coffee. It was hard to get past the feeling that this Christmas was going to suck. Michael didn't pin much on the idea of some days being more special than others, but Christmas day was at least supposed to be happy. It had been over the last several years, when Chris and Michael spent the holiday together. Of course, it hadn't been the case when Chris and Michael were growing up.

Christmas had always been a strange day in the Kelly household. Dad was nice on Christmas, almost too nice. But as was typical for him, he had a very strong sense of the way things should be, and Christmas was tailor-made for him since it was supposed to be perfect. Dad liked perfect and hated everything else. He was affectionate with Mom on Christmas, putting his arm around her and kissing her on the temple. She soaked up every minute of it, probably because it was not their normal dynamic at all. Christmas was essentially a day for a cease-fire. His parents' marriage seemed more like a hostile business arrangement, a constant negotiation and a relentless power struggle. The only thing that kept Dad in line was that Mom held the purse strings.

Most of the family's money came from an inheritance Mom had received from her aunt when Michael was eight and Chris was six. Before that, finances had always been tight. In some ways, they'd had a happier home life before the money came along. Dad worked, which meant their exposure to his short fuse and perfectionism was lessened. Swimming was an activity driven by the boys, fueled by their love of being in the water and competing. But when the money came, Dad quit his job and he funneled every waking minute into Michael and Chris.

They were plucked from their schools and their friends, the family moved from a modest ranch in rural Maryland to a massive historic home in Bethesda. Dad had the entire backyard ripped out, two-hundred-year-old trees and all, just so they could put in a pool. A private swimming coach was hired, but only one who was willing to let Dad attend practice and micromanage everything. Their old life, which wasn't perfect but was manageable, became a distant memory. Their new life became a living hell because the bar had been raised significantly. Their parents had changed everyone's lives in order to create two Olympians. Any result short of that would be an utter failure. The pressure was on. If Michael and Chris hadn't had each other, he wasn't sure they would have made it.

Michael poured himself a cup of coffee and wandered into the living room, sinking into the couch cushions and getting lost in his view out the window. It was a gray and overcast day with more snow predicted. After a while, he wasn't sure how long he'd been sitting there, only that his coffee had gone cold. Abby was curled up with her head on his lap, sleeping fitfully, her nose and front paws twitching. "Chasing rabbits in your sleep, sweets?" he asked, smoothing his hand over her silky fur.

"You talking to the dog again?" Chris shuffled into the room, his eyes about half-open.

"I would've been talking to you, but you're the one who decided to sleep in."

Chris rubbed his face and squinted when the sun peeked out from behind a cloud, flooding the room with light. "We drank too much last night, dude."

Michael was still feeling rough, but apparently not as bad as his brother. "I had to give you a chance to beat me at cards. I didn't want you going home with your pride completely destroyed."

"Yeah, yeah." Chris waved it off. "We could've played without doing shots until midnight. That was your idea."

I was drowning my sorrows. "Coffee's on." Michael nodded toward the kitchen and Chris ambled off.

His brother returned a minute later and plopped

down at the other end of the couch. "It's been a full twenty-four hours since you came back from Charlotte's apartment. We successfully avoided the subject all day yesterday, but I think your reprieve is over. You want to tell me what in the hell happened? Because you seem just as bummed out this morning as you did all day yesterday."

What in the hell *had* happened? Michael still couldn't make sense of it. Everything had snowballed so quickly. He didn't make a habit of spilling his guts to his brother, but Chris was a great listener and he really needed someone to help him sort this out. "As long as you're sure you want to hear this. I'm pretty sure I messed up and I'm not sure how to fix it."

"I will always listen, but especially if it involves you messing up." He bounced his eyebrows and took a long sip of his coffee.

"Well, things were pretty intense after you left the party the other night."

"I know I probably shouldn't have said anything, but she's the only woman you've talked about since the engagement and she cares about you a lot."

Michael wasn't sure that could be true, or at least not anymore. The disdain in her eyes had come from such a pure place yesterday, and he wasn't sure he blamed her. "I'm not so sure after yesterday." Michael craned his neck to work out a kink. The whole story was tumbling around in his head—every mistake he'd made, the way he kept stubbornly clinging to his own baggage. "But I'm glad you said something. As much as I didn't want her to know about my past, I do feel like it broke down some barriers between us."

"Good. That all sounds great."

"When we woke up yesterday morning, it felt like we were in a different place. A much better place than we'd been when we were together the first time." Just thinking about waking up next to her stirred up emotions that were most often foreign to Michael—optimism, hope, peace. Charlotte was such a positive force in his life when they were on the same trajectory. Little had he known he was throwing it away by being so damn shortsighted.

"Again. This all sounds good to me."

"It was." Michael clunked his empty coffee mug on the side table next to him. "Then she took her dog for a walk and I found prenatal vitamins on her bathroom counter. She's pregnant." Michael looked over at his brother, and watched the news sink in.

"Wow. Who's the dad?"

Michael recalled this part of the conversation with Charlotte. He was starting to wonder why he'd ever thought *he* was the smart one. "It's me. She got pregnant when we were still together, but she didn't find out until after we broke up."

Chris ran his hands through his hair, shaking his head. "Oh, wow. That is so harsh. Finding out you're pregnant by some guy who told you he had no interest in being serious? That had to hurt."

Michael had spent much of last night tipsy and trying to imagine how Charlotte must have felt right after their breakup and during her time in England. She'd been suffering and he'd been going on with his own life, missing her, which had seemed like a big step forward in his own emotional growth. Little did he know she was running laps around him. "Yeah. I'm guessing it hurt a lot. But that didn't really occur to me yesterday. I was too mad at her for keeping it from me."

"Are you serious? Mad?" He turned on the couch, facing Michael more directly.

"Yes. I'm not proud of it. At all."

"So did she give you the heave-ho? Is that why you've been in such a terrible mood?"

"Not right away. I told her I needed time to think about it, she got mad, which is understandable, and I left." Michael sighed and shook his head. What an idiot he'd been. "But then she went after me in the hall." Michael went on to explain Charlotte's ultimatum about one of them moving out. Abby woke up and nudged Michael's hand with her nose. "Human relationships are too complicated, Abs. I like what we have. I feed you, take you for a walk, you're excited when I get home from work. Easy."

"Look, Dad did a number on both of us," Chris said. "I know that everything with your engagement convinced you life would be easier if you didn't get serious with a woman, and I understand that, but you need to get your priorities straight. Charlotte is amazing and she's going to have your baby. Don't sit in your apartment petting your dog and talking to your brother. That's not you. You should be down the hall working this out with her."

"I tried. I keep texting her and she doesn't answer. I went down to her apartment and knocked on her door last night when you ran out for more beer, but there was no answer."

"Maybe she's doing something with her family."

"We still have big issues to deal with once she finally talks to me. What about a baby? What if I ruin everything? What if I've inherited Dad's parenting skills? I'm just as competitive. I'm just as much of a perfectionist. I don't want to do to my child what he did to us."

"Hey. You need to cut that out, now. Neither of us is Dad."

"You didn't see me yesterday. I just couldn't let go of the fact that she'd deceived me. I was so hung up on her being wrong and me being right that I couldn't see straight. It was right out of Dad's playbook."

Chris shook his head. "And what's going on right here? This conversation? This is definitely not something Dad would ever do. He never questioned his actions. You're not him, Michael. You just aren't."

Was that really true? Michael wanted to believe it. He did. "I need to figure out a way to fix this." It always stung to admit defeat, but Michael found that he felt better when he committed himself to making things better.

"Any ideas?"

He picked up his phone and again tormented himself with the unanswered texts. "I need to talk to her. That's still my first step." He might be scared out of his wits and totally unsure of himself, but he had to do right by Charlotte. He had to go back to the way he'd felt before he found out about the pregnancy. The moment when he'd been ready to tell her he loved her. "I'm going back down to her apartment again."

"Good idea. I'll hold down the fort."

Michael got up and headed straight down the hall, hoping the second time would be the charm. He wanted to try to make this work. He wanted to take on the challenge ahead, however daunting. It was funny to think that every other big challenge he'd ever tackled had at least come after unbelievable amounts of preparation. Not today. He was flying as blind as could be. Or maybe all those years of suffering at his father's hand had prepared him, but not in the way one normally does that sort of thing.

He reached Charlotte's door and knocked. He waited, tapping his foot, looking down at the floor, up at the ceiling, back at the door again. There was no answer. He leaned closer and held his ear to the door. Not a sound came from her apartment. He knocked a second time, this time a bit more forcefully. Not even a yip from Thor came in response. He had to redouble his efforts. He dug his phone out of his back pocket and sent her yet another text.

You home? I'm in the hall. Hoping we can talk.

He stared at his phone. The silence and the non-answer began to eat at him. He wasn't sure where Charlotte was—on the other side of that door or off somewhere celebrating the holiday. But no matter what, he was quite certain she was mad as hell.

As he made his way down the hall, his brain went into work mode. If Charlotte was going to be stubborn and ignore him, he was going to have to get creative. He was going to have to get her attention. He was going to have to call Sawyer.

Charlotte didn't want to spend Christmas in utter despair, but it seemed that things were going to be that way. After the breakup to end all breakups the day before, she had zero confidence this would be a merry Christmas. *Ho ho ho and deck the halls, my butt.* Maybe next year. Next year could be merry. A baby. A career. An apartment, exact location to be determined. She could live with that. However imperfect, it would be a hell of a lot better than things had been before she met Michael.

Sawyer had invited Charlotte, Fran and Noah over for an early dinner. That left Charlotte to spend

Christmas morning in bed, sleeping, even after she'd turned in very early the night before. She'd turned off her phone. She'd put earplugs in her ears. No rushing to the tree and opening gifts with loved ones while sipping hot cocoa or eggnog. It was just her and Thor curled up into a pathetic ball, a good deal of crying and a few fits of anger. She'd not only managed to lose Michael, the man she had an inexplicable weakness for, but she'd also managed to lose the father of her child. In a life littered with tragic mistakes, this one went to Number One with a bullet on the top-ten list of self-made disasters. It would undoubtedly stay there for eternity.

Going to Sawyer's place might've seemed like nothing more complicated than a friendly family gathering, but it was, in truth, a day of reckoning, when Charlotte had just lived through one. Charlotte hadn't spoken to Sawyer since the day after the wedding, when they'd all had breakfast before he and Kendall escaped to Miami for a few days. He would expect a sales update today, and although the report wasn't terrible, she hadn't reached her goal, either. She'd boasted that she would sell her apartments first, but she'd fallen behind Michael. He had one unit left, she had two. It didn't sound like much, but they weren't selling lollipops or I Love NY T-shirts. They were selling multimillion-dollar pieces of real estate. Two wealthy buyers were unlikely to suddenly appear in Charlotte's life.

Fran and Charlotte took a car together for the short ride up to Sawyer's apartment on the Upper West Side. Fran had let Charlotte bend her ear about Michael yesterday, and although she was glad Charlotte had stood up for herself, she was also very clear about two things—first, she needed to cool off for a few days, and second, she needed to finally just tell her family about the baby. No more waiting until she finished her sales. It was Christmas Day, and if anything was welcome today, it was good news. A baby certainly fell into the category of good news.

Noah was already there when they got up to Sawyer's. He took Charlotte's and Fran's coats, then everyone settled in the living room for predinner drinks.

"I love what you've done with the apartment," Charlotte said to Kendall. "It's much homier now."

"Was it not homey before?" Sawyer asked, seeming a bit insulted.

"It was always nice. Don't get me wrong. But it's nicer now with the new throw pillows on the couch and the candles on the coffee table."

Sawyer shrugged. "Sorry, but it never really occurred to me that I needed more pillows."

"See? That's why you needed Kendall." Charlotte smiled at her new sister-in-law, whom she officially adored. It was nice not to be the only girl, and Fran would be going back to England soon, so Kendall might end up being Charlotte's only real ally. With two babies between them, they'd probably have a lot to talk about.

"So, what can I get everyone to drink?" Sawyer asked, rubbing his hands together. "I'm thinking a Manhattan."

"Yes, please." Fran thrust her hand up into the air. Sawyer was speaking her language.

"Sounds good to me," Noah said.

"Water for me," Kendall said.

"Charlotte?"

She'd known her turn at her brother's question was coming, but the words were stuck in her throat. Something was apparently also stuck in Fran's throat—she cleared it in a way that could only suggest she was thinking, *Charlotte, just come out with it.*

"I will have the same as Kendall. Just water, please."

"It's not like you to pass up cocktail hour, Charlotte."

No, it wasn't. "That's because I have some news." She sat straighter in her seat and looked at each member of her family, one by one. Noah, Sawyer, Fran, Kendall. This was her support system. This was the extent of it. Every person she could absolutely count on was in this room. Michael was now strictly in the category of people she could not count on. "I'm pregnant."

What came next was a squeal from Kendall, a nervous and somewhat unwarranted laugh from Noah, enthusiastic clapping from Fran and a dumbfounded "wow" from Sawyer. She wasn't sure what to make of her family's response and she wasn't about to go around the room and ask each individual for their opinion. "I'm about to start my second trimester. Things are going well, and I'm very excited about what the future holds for me."

Kendall got up from her chair and took the empty seat on the sofa between Charlotte and Fran. She pulled Charlotte's hand into her lap and looked into her eyes sweetly. "I think it's wonderful. There will be two baby Lockes running around. They can play together and grow up together. Cousins. It will be amazing."

A picture materialized before Charlotte's eyes, one that she hadn't thought about—the baby as a toddler, a cousin, an actual person. She'd been so wrapped up in the notion of a little bundle, swaddled in a baby blanket. She'd thought only of cribs and diapers and sleepless nights. It hit her like a ton of bricks, exactly what was at stake. She would be responsible for a human for the rest of her life. It would be her job not to screw it up. Charlotte, the perpetual screwup herself. And then there was the most damning detail—this baby would be a Locke. He or she would not be a Kelly.

The tears started to flow and Charlotte couldn't

have stopped them if she'd wanted to. It was surprising to say the least. She'd spent her whole morning crying. How could she possibly have any tears left? Maybe it was because she had been under so much stress with work or maybe it was as simple as what had prompted it—a glimpse of the future.

Kendall plaintively looked up at Sawyer. "I don't know what I said, but I'm so sorry."

Charlotte dropped her head onto Kendall's shoulder. "No. No. It's fine. I'm just still coming to terms with everything and trying to sort stuff out." Good God, this was exactly like the speech Charlotte had delivered every other time in her life that she'd messed up. How was it that she was still repeating this pattern? "And I should let you guys know that I've known for a while now. That's why I went to England to see Fran. I needed some time to regroup and figure out what my next step would be."

Sawyer walked across the room and dropped to his knee next to Charlotte. "Why wouldn't you tell us, Charlotte? We're your family. This is a big deal."

Noah stood directly behind Sawyer, his face full of concern. Things like this were difficult for Noah. He'd never been much for drama. Fran, Charlotte's fairy godmother, wore a reassuring smile that held an edge of "I told you so."

"I've spent my whole life as the member of the family who's constantly messing things up. I didn't want to be that person anymore. Getting pregnant seemed too much like classic Charlotte. I really wanted the chance to prove myself first by selling my units at the Grand Legacy, then I was going to tell you all."

"Prove yourself?" Sawyer asked. "Charlotte, you're my sister. I love you. You don't have to prove a thing to me."

"That's not true and you know it. I saw the hesitation on your face that morning I came in and asked for the listings. You weren't convinced I could do it. You still aren't convinced."

"If I had any hesitation at all, it was only because I could see you doubting yourself. I never want you to doubt yourself, Charlotte. You're far more resilient than me or Noah."

Charlotte let out an unflattering snort. "Yeah, right. Resilient is the last thing I am. Look at me. I'm a mess."

Sawyer shook his head. "I'm not kidding. You roll with the punches and you've had some doozies to deal with. You always had a harder time when we were growing up. You always manage to find your way through everything, and you make everyone love you while you're doing it. You might be the only member of the Locke family who doesn't have an enemy."

Charlotte laughed quietly, wiping tears from her cheeks with the back of her hands. "Yeah, I guess."

"No, he's right," Noah insisted. "As awful as Dad has been to us, he was worse with you. He ignored you like crazy. I'm sure that had to sting."

Just then Charlotte realized perhaps why it had hurt so deeply when Michael ignored her or didn't give her the attention she wanted. It wasn't just because she was a bottomless vessel for love and affection. Michael was just a continuation of a persistent theme in her life. She loved him and he didn't love her back.

"Do you want to tell us who the dad is?" Sawyer asked. "I mean, you don't have to if you don't want to. I guess I just want to know what your plans are." He turned back to Noah. "I think both of us want to know what you need from us. If someone needs to fill in."

"Yes. Of course," Noah agreed.

Charlotte examined Sawyer's face. He was such a sweet guy. She was a lucky girl to have him as her brother. Noah, too. "It's Michael Kelly, Sawyer. I got pregnant when we were still a couple. I know this makes it one hundred times more complicated, but I assure you that I have everything in hand. I'm working on it." *Even if it ends up being nothing.*

Sawyer closed his eyes for a moment. "You do not skimp on the surprise factor, do you?"

Charlotte managed a small grin. "I try not to. Makes life more exciting."

"Wait a minute. Is that why he gave you the listing on his one unsold unit?" Sawyer asked.

"What are you talking about?" Charlotte wasn't sure she'd heard her brother correctly.

"Michael. He called me around noon today and said he was giving his one remaining listing to you. He said he would work it out with you once he got a hold of you. He told me he'd been trying to reach you by text, but you weren't answering."

Crap. Charlotte dug her phone out of her bag and powered it up. She'd been running behind when Fran came to her apartment before the car arrived. She hadn't looked at her phone at all. There on the screen was a whole string of texts and missed calls from him. What did this mean? Did he want to talk because he wanted to reconcile? Giving up the listing made no sense. Unless he was simply taking pity on her.

"Excuse me. I need to freshen up." Charlotte tucked her phone back into her purse and made her way to the hall powder room. Her stomach felt all kinds of uneasy. She couldn't figure out what her response to Michael should be. Did he have something up his sleeve? Or should she stop being so paranoid? With that thought came a sharp pain. When she wiped, she found an unwanted surprise—blood on the tissue. She tried not to panic, but her heart was beating as fast as it could. She washed her hands, but they were trembling under the steady stream of water. She could hardly rub them together to work up a lather. She had to call the doctor. She might have to go in.

She rushed out of the bathroom and back to the living room. Getting in touch with Michael would have to wait. "Fran, Kendall, can I talk to you for a minute?" One thing was certain. Charlotte might have a knack for making life more exciting, but this might go down as the most disastrous Christmas yet.

Thirteen

Michael's cell phone rang and he jumped. *Charlotte?* He flipped his phone over, disappointment sinking into his belly for what felt like the hundredth time today. It wasn't Charlotte, but he didn't recognize the number, either. That wasn't entirely unusual. He received cold calls all the time, but it was late on Christmas day, not a typical time for real-estate inquiries from strangers.

"Hey, Chris. I'm going to take this." Michael and his brother were watching a movie. It was supposed to be a distraction from the Charlotte situation, even if Michael's mind kept wandering. His brain insisted on ruminating, dragging every misstep he'd made into plain view.

"You want me to pause it?" Chris asked.

"No. It's okay." He got up from the couch and walked into the kitchen. "Hello?"

"Michael. This is Charlotte's aunt, Fran. I need to speak with you." She was practically whispering. Whatever she was calling about, something was wrong. He could hear it in her voice.

"Yes. Of course. What's going on?"

"I'm at the hospital. With Charlotte."

Forget how grave and serious everything had seemed when he'd discovered Charlotte was pregnant with his child. The hospital? Had she been in an accident? "What happened?"

"She started bleeding. The doctors asked for one of us to bring her in so she could be checked. We were over at Sawyer's for dinner when it started."

Michael felt as though everything in his body had just gone cold. He couldn't believe he'd spent even a minute today moping around, feeling sorry for himself. "Is she okay?" He wasn't even sure what to ask about the baby. It was still such an abstract idea. Charlotte was hardly showing. If he hadn't seen the vitamins on the bathroom counter, he might not even know right now. Charlotte had been that good at keeping the secret from him.

"Charlotte seems very worried. She could be losing the baby. It's still early in the pregnancy. It wouldn't be uncommon."

Michael felt his body go incredibly still, his breathing slowed and his pulse felt like it was fading. How did it feel to have something go from an abstract idea to a reality in the blink of an eye? Michael was feeling exactly that right now. "Tell me where you are. I have to be there if anything happens."

"Oh, thank God. I'm so happy to hear you say that."

There was no telling what Charlotte had said about him to Fran, but he had a strong inkling now. "I care about Charlotte very much. But I am a little concerned about whether or not she wants me there. I don't want to come down if it's going to upset her. I'm no doctor, but I'm guessing it's probably best for her and the baby if she stays calm."

"You'll have to trust me when I say that it will be much worse if you don't come."

Michael wasn't sure what that even meant, but he didn't want to discuss it further. "I'm on my way out the door right now. Can you text me the address?"

He and Fran said their goodbyes, he grabbed his fleece jacket and hat, then poked his head into the living room. "I'd love to stick around and try to explain this, but I have to go. Charlotte's in the hospital. There's a chance she might lose the baby." He headed for the door.

"Michael, wait. Do you want me to come with you?"

"I'll call you if we need anything, but otherwise, I need to do this on my own. I'm sorry to bail on you."

The concern was so plain on Chris's face it nearly broke Michael's heart. "Don't be silly. Abby and I will be fine. But are you really going to go dressed like that?"

Michael looked down at himself. He'd completely forgotten that he was wearing shorts and a sweatshirt. "Yeah. It's fine. I don't want to take the time to change."

"And it's snowing, you know."

The text from Fran came through with the hospital address. It was only a few blocks away. "Yeah. It's fine. I think I'm going to run. I'll get there faster than driving."

"You're certifiable, bro."

"I love her, Chris. There's nothing else for me to do."

Michael didn't bother with the elevator, and flew down the Grand Legacy stairwell. He tore through the lobby, nearly knocking over a bellman, and bolted out onto the street. He hit the pavement at full stride, his long legs carrying him as fast as he could possibly go. The icy air stabbed at his lungs, but no speed other than lightning-fast would have seemed right. He had to get there now. He had to get there an hour ago. His brain was running just as fast. *Please be okay. Please be okay.* The thought of her being anything less than perfectly safe and healthy made his stomach lurch. In that moment, he knew not only that he loved Charlotte, but that he also wanted things to work out between them. He wanted them to be together. No, she hadn't answered a single one of his text messages. Didn't matter. He still had to try.

Fran had said that Charlotte was up on the third floor in Labor and Delivery, which sounded like a scary proposition. The baby had to be tiny. How could it have come to this already? He ran in through the main entrance. The hospital was eerily quiet, so much so that it felt like his breathing was unreasonably loud. The information desk was empty, and no one offered to direct him, which he decided was for the best. Christmas was apparently not a popular day at the hospital.

Again, he took the stairs instead of the elevator. Fran was waiting for him out in the hall.

"How's she doing?" He was huffing and puffing. His cheeks were burning.

Fran looked as though she'd aged five years since the last time Michael had seen her, which was only at Sawyer's wedding. "They have a monitor on her. They've picked up the baby's heartbeat, so that's a good sign. They want to watch her for a few more hours. They're hoping the bleeding will stop on its own."

Michael swallowed hard. He was used to dealing with all sorts of crises with work, but life and death were not a regular part of his day. "Can I see her?"

Fran nodded. "Yes. I'll walk you in."

He followed her down the hall. The hospital was

certainly nicer than most he'd been to, but nobody ever chose to be here. There was no avoiding the overwhelming sense of that. Fran pushed open the door and Michael trailed her into the room. Charlotte was to his left, lying on her side, both hands tucked under her head. Her eyes were closed. She was wearing a blue-and-white hospital gown. The vision left him even more uneasy than he'd imagined it would.

"Charlotte, darling," Fran whispered. "Are you awake?"

Charlotte's eyes popped open. The instant she saw Michael, she jerked up to a sitting position. "Michael? You came?" Her eyes homed in on Fran. "Did you call him?"

Fran sat on the edge of the bed and gently pushed on Charlotte's arm until she relented and laid back down. "I called him because he's the father and he should be involved in this."

Charlotte shook her head. "You don't have to be here if you don't want to. Honestly, I don't want you here at all if you're only here out of obligation."

Michael blew out a breath. He'd earned that response. "I'm here because I want to be here. I'm glad Fran called me." He dared to step closer. Charlotte's eyes slowly went from fiercely guarded to merely skeptical. He'd take what he could get. "She's worried about you. And quite frankly, I'm worried, too."

A faint scowl crossed Charlotte's face. "I hope

you didn't just come for brownie points. Or to make yourself look good."

"Never." Apparently she still thought he was capable of the worst. "I'm more of a chocolate-chip-cookie guy anyway."

She narrowed her beautiful blue eyes. "Stop trying to be clever."

"And stop arguing with me. However little I know about having a baby or being pregnant, I'm guessing that the doctor has told you to rest and relax."

Fran cast her sights up at him, then back at Charlotte. "He's right, darling. And I didn't call him to upset you. I called him because everything between you two is going to need to get worked out at some point and the sooner we start, the better for everyone. Even if it ends up being nothing more than a truce." Fran got up from the bed and smoothed the rumpled sheets. "Now I'm going in search of a decent cup of coffee. I'll leave you two to talk."

Michael watched as Fran disappeared through the door, unsure of where his fate sat in all of this. Usually, when he and Charlotte talked, things did *not* get straightened out. They typically became that much more tangled. Considering everything that had happened in the last forty-eight hours, he decided there was no way things could get any worse.

Charlotte couldn't believe Fran had interfered. Although, if the roles and been reversed, Charlotte probably would've done the exact same thing. Even that was hard to believe—it was always Charlotte in the role of being the person in a pickle. It was her job to star as the screwup in the Locke family drama, shows nightly and two matinees on the weekend.

Right now, she was about as stuck as could be. Pregnant by the hopelessly handsome guy standing next to her hospital bed who had shown little desire in being a father, which was such a shame. Michael Kelly was too hot to be a sperm donor. Maybe she needed to just be thankful that he'd given her his exceptional genetic material. If everything turned out, this baby she was already so attached to, the child she wanted more than anything, would be beautiful, strong and smart. And much of that would be thanks to Michael.

"May I?" Michael gestured to the chair next to the bed. Apparently, he was staying for a while, which actually sounded nice, even if he wasn't her favorite person right now.

"Yes. Of course."

"Thanks." He dragged it closer, his knees meeting the mattress when he sat.

"You're wearing shorts? It's December. And snowing."

He sat back and crossed his hairy legs. The man's genetic gifts were off-the-charts, but his legs might be the crowning touch—a million miles long, every muscle as strong as a horse. "This is what I was wearing when Fran called. And I figured running was the best way to get here."

"So you're all sweaty and gross under that jacket."

He nodded. "Afraid so."

"Yuck."

Michael laughed and shook his head. "I already knew there was no winning in that scenario. Show up in basketball shorts and get crap for it, or take the time to change and get crap for that." He folded his arms across his chest and looked her in the eye, wagging his foot at the same time. "So I stayed in the dumbest clothes possible for December in New York, left my car back at the Grand Legacy and ran right over."

"You ran in the snow. To the hospital. To see me." Charlotte zeroed in on his face. It was never a simple matter to look at him. There was too much wrapped up in that incredible package. Maybe he did deserve some brownie points. "Thank you for doing that. It was very chivalrous of you."

"You had to know I would never let you down when it came to the important stuff."

She sucked in a deep breath. Did he mean *every* important thing? "That was always my hope."

"So what are the doctors saying?"

Charlotte's hand instinctively went to her belly. "They want me to stay on the monitor for a few hours, although I think what they're mostly trying to do is keep me in this bed and off my feet. Unfortunately, there's not a lot they can do at this point if my body decides to…" The word got stuck in her throat. Tiny tears stung her eyes. She didn't want to think it. She didn't want to lend the thought any credence. Too much of her life had been worrying about the worst-case scenario, only to have it come true. "You know. If the pregnancy isn't viable." Using the more clinical term was of zero comfort. If anything, it made her feel worse.

He went for quite a while without saying anything. This was probably just too much for Michael to deal with. She'd have to go with assuming that. She didn't want to imagine him having anything else on his mind. He sat forward and rested his elbows on his knees, reaching for her hand. "Then I will stay until they decide you can go home."

"You don't have to do that. Fran should be back in a little bit and I'll be fine. I know this isn't really your scene, Michael. I know this is a lot for you to deal with and you never asked for any of it."

He wrinkled his nose and pressed his lips together, staring off through the picture window on the far side of the room. It was one of the most powerful shows of emotion she'd ever seen from Michael. Normally he was so composed, so in control. Perhaps it was just an illustration of how difficult this was for him. "I want to be here with you. The thought of leaving you makes me feel like my chest is being hollowed out."

"I definitely don't want you to feel like that."

He looked at her, gazing into her eyes, but it wasn't like he was peeling back her layers. It was more like he was peeling back his own. She saw a vulnerable man behind those cool blue eyes, one with no agenda. He wasn't calculating or planning. He was the most in the moment she'd ever seen him. He raised her hand to his lips and brushed her skin with a tender kiss. "I just want to be here for you."

"And the baby?" She hated that there was so much hope pinned to her question. It felt like a plea she was throwing into the wind, knowing very well that it could fly right back into her face.

"And the baby. Of course, the baby."

There was a stiffness to his voice and a hardness in his face that she disliked so much she would've done almost anything to make it go away. Tiny victories, she decided. Michael had shown up, looking like hell, no less, which was more like a normal day for most people. Six months ago, she would've killed for this much attention from Michael.

"Do you want to tell me why you called Sawyer and told him you were giving up your final listing? Does that mean you want to move out?"

He shook his head. "No. I don't want to move out. And I don't want you to move out, either. I figured you were just trying to get my attention, and I had to figure out a way to get yours. I know you tell me I'm fixated on work too much, but you've been guilty of the same over the last few weeks."

"I know. I was just trying to cement my future and the baby's."

"I still wish you would've let me be a part of that."

That familiar and deep sense of regret rolled back over her, but she took it as it came. There was nothing to do about it now. "I know. I messed up."

He leaned closer and took her hand. "You know what? We both messed up. I kept a secret from you, too. When we were together the first time around, I should've opened up to you. I know now that you were trying to get me to do exactly that. Every day. Every nice thing you ever did for me. I just fought it."

"Because of your family? Because of everything Chris told me?"

"Honestly, I think part of me felt like I wasn't good enough for you."

"How could you ever think that?" Charlotte couldn't fathom the idea. He was so extraordinary.

"I was so afraid of being weak. I was terrified of being at a disadvantage or putting myself in a position to lose. I didn't want you to see every fault in me." He reached out and brushed the hair from the side of her face. It was then that she could see tears misting in his eyes. "It's what I always do. I put on that perfect front and I hide the mistakes because I've learned to hate them. I've been taught to hate every imperfect part of me. But I can't live like that anymore. I messed up yesterday morning. I'm not the jerky guy who blamed everything on you. I'm really not."

Charlotte choked back her own tears. In her heart of hearts, she'd hoped Michael wasn't really the guy who would push her away. "I know you're not. I never truly thought you were. I was just mad."

"I love you, Charlotte. And I'm not just saying that because you're in a hospital bed and our future feels like it's hanging in the balance. I'm saying it now because I can't spend another minute of my life knowing that I'm not sharing everything inside of me with you."

Oh, good God, how she'd longed to hear words like those. She smiled wide. "I love you, too. I was going to tell you the night we broke up. I've loved you for a long time."

"Honestly, I think I've loved you from the moment we became a couple. I couldn't admit it to myself because it meant casting aside the facade that made it easy for me to succeed."

"What changed?"

He laughed quietly, but she could see the sadness in his eyes. "You. You're what's changed me. What's changed me is walking into this room and seeing you in this bed and knowing that you are as vulnerable as a person can be and you're still you. You make me want to be a better man, Charlie. You make me want to be the real, imperfect Michael Kelly."

"Only slightly imperfect. Look at you."

He pushed his chair aside and kneeled beside the bed. He clutched her hand tightly, squeezing. "I love you, Charlotte. I mean it. I love you and I want us to be a family. I want us to build a life together. Please tell me we will try to find a way to make this work."

"I love you, too, Michael." She loved seeing the relief on his face, the way his soft eyes became impossibly warm. She could look at his glorious face forever. It would always make her feel at least a little bit invincible. "If you're willing to make it work, I am, too. We're both pretty stubborn, so I think we can take a good run at it if we're on the same side."

"I never want to be on opposite sides with you again, Charlie. That's a surefire way to lose."

Fourteen

The bleeding didn't stop, so the doctors decided it was best for Charlotte to stay overnight. Michael didn't leave her side. He told Fran to go home and get some sleep. There was no point in everyone being exhausted, he'd said. He touched base with Sawyer and let him know what was going on. The nurse brought him a blanket and he moved his chair so he could sit right alongside Charlotte, holding her hand all night long.

In the morning, she woke to a note.

Charlie,
Gone in search of coffee. Be back soon.
Love, Michael

She smiled to herself, feeling a pretty big sense of pride. She'd trained Michael Kelly to do something that fell squarely in the category of quality boyfriend behavior. Now to get herself to the bathroom.

She hadn't told Michael, since he'd been asleep and the nurse said there was no way they would discharge her in the middle of the night, but the bleeding had considerably lessened when she'd gone to the bathroom around 4:00 a.m. Fingers crossed they were on the right trajectory, that this was just a minor bump in the road. They'd had enough roadblocks. She wanted to look ahead to their future.

Sure enough, the tissue this morning had been only the tiniest bit of pink. She came out of the bathroom and a new nurse who had just come on duty was waiting for her. "That's perfectly normal. Sounds like somebody gets to go home," she said after Charlotte gave her the report.

Michael popped in a minute later. The nurse turned and was instantly awestruck, either by his handsomeness or his ridiculous height or the fact that an Olympian was standing in the room.

"Hi. Michael Kelly." He shook her hand, but she couldn't manage much of a response other than a goofy grin before she cleared out of the room so Charlotte could get dressed.

"They're letting me go home," she said. "No real bleeding since the middle of the night."

"Really?" The hopefulness in his voice was so raw and real.

"Really." She turned her back to him. "Can you untie this gown, please? I can't wait to get out of this thing."

"Gladly." He did as promised, but then he snaked his arms around her bare waist, sending a million tiny jolts of electricity through her. He pulled her back against his chest and kissed the top of her head, then her neck, making her head swim with possibilities.

"No hospital sex."

"I wouldn't think of it. Just feeling like I should take advantage of your semidressed state."

"Always a flirt." She turned and swatted him on the arm, then grabbed his shoulders and urged him down to her level for a quick kiss. "But I love it."

Charlotte dressed with a running commentary from Michael about how impressive her breasts were now and that if he'd known that was a side effect of pregnancy, he would've been on board with it from the very beginning.

After Charlotte signed her discharge papers, an orderly arrived with a wheelchair for her. Michael insisted on pushing.

"I feel really dumb in this thing," Charlotte said, taking a seat. "I'm perfectly capable of walking downstairs."

"The nurse said it's a rule. Plus, it's giving me good practice for after the baby arrives."

Contentment crept over her, but she just went along for the ride. Michael pushed her through the electric doors once they were down to the ground floor. He parked the wheelchair to the side.

"You're being so normal about this whole thing. I'm kind of amazed," she said.

"You know me. Once I'm on board with something, I want to be the best. That would be the good side of my competitive nature."

Charlotte had to smile. "Are we walking?"

"It's up to you. It's only four or five blocks, but I'm happy to hail a cab if that makes you feel better."

"Michael Kelly taking a cab? My stars, you have changed."

"I'm just trying to keep you happy."

"Good answer." She hooked her arm in his. "I vote we walk. I feel like I've been cooped up inside forever."

They started off on their walk and Charlotte was overcome with a feeling that was both unfamiliar and wonderful. She had stability. She and Michael had worked past his problems and hers. She'd made her mark in business, and she'd come to better understand the ways her brothers perceived her. She could officially stop thinking of herself as the family goof-up. From now on, she could just be Charlotte, the real-estate agent. Or the little sister. Or the new mom. Possibly Michael Kelly's wife, although she wasn't ready to put the thumbscrews on him yet about that. She'd give him a week or two to propose and then she'd reevaluate.

"You know," she began, "I know you were trying to help me, but I now have three more units to sell instead of two. You just ended up making more work for me."

"I was thinking about that." He snugged her closer and put his arm around her as they stopped at a corner and waited for the walk signal. "Not necessarily. I got a text from Alan this morning. The guy from the party? He's ready to buy. He wants that last unit on seventeen."

"Oh, wow."

"I told him to contact you about it. I hope that's okay. I gave him your number, but asked him to hold off on calling you for a few days. I want you to get your rest."

The light turned green, and they made their way across the street, hand in hand. "Are you sure? Every sale you turn down is one more chance for Gabe Underwood to unseat you as top agent in the city next year."

"I couldn't possibly care less about Gabe. If he ends up on top, that's fine. I'll just have to beat his butt the next year. And for all I know, you're going to be the one to beat me."

"That's right. You'd better watch your back, Kelly." Charlotte squeezed his hand a little harder. "That leaves the two units on our floor. We're going to have to be careful about those. I really don't want some jerky neighbor living next to us. But before that…" She stopped herself there. Michael had said he wanted to try, but that was all he'd said, and she didn't want to be the one to put any pressure on him. The man knew very well how to put himself in the hot seat. She was fine simply moving forward as a couple, taking things one day at a time.

"Before that, we have to decide if we're going to live in your apartment or mine," he said, with no prompting from Charlotte at all.

She was a little relieved Michael wasn't looking at her right now. The grin that popped onto her face would've been embarrassing. How happy she was to be on the same page. "Right. Do you have any thoughts about that?" She looked up to see him deep in thought, bobbing his head, something he did a lot when he was thinking.

"I hope this doesn't sound crazy, but I just don't think one apartment is enough. I mean, Abby needs her space. We both know Thor needs room to roam. We might even be able to convince him that he's still escaping, but we could just let him into another room."

Charlotte laughed. "I'd like to think he's too smart for that, but I'm not sure." She started to think out their options. "Are you thinking two units? And we knock down a wall in between?"

He shrugged. "I don't know. How many kids do you want?"

She stepped in front of him and held up a hand. He stopped cold in his tracks. "Hold on. How many kids? Are you sure you're feeling okay? Right now, I'm pretty stuck on the idea of one kid and we re-evaluate later."

He leaned down and kissed her nose. "I feel great. But you know me. I'm a planner. I don't do anything halfway." He held up his finger, a sign he was about to make an important point. "Which brings me to the wedding."

"The wedding?"

"I know. This sucks. We're standing on a sidewalk in New York and I'm still wearing shorts from yesterday. This isn't the way I would've planned this at all. But in a day or two, when you're feeling better, I'd like to take you to pick out a ring so I can get down on one knee in some place other than a hospital room, profess my love for you and ask you to marry me."

"Wow." Charlotte nearly asked him to pinch her. If it wasn't so cold out, she would've thought she was dreaming.

"You are planning on saying yes, aren't you?" He narrowed his vision on her and one of his arrogant smirks crossed his face. "I feel like I can see the gears turning in your head."

"Yes, Michael Kelly. I'm planning on saying yes. As long as you're on your best behavior until then."

"There's always something with you, isn't there?" He took her hand. "Come on. My legs are freezing."

A block later, they arrived in front of the Grand Legacy. Something about the moment warranted a stop and a look up at the building, in all its beautiful glory. The Christmas decorations were still up, the heavy swags of pine and the red-and-gold garland. It wouldn't be long before they'd be ringing in the New Year in the Grand Legacy. "I love the hotel, Michael. It really is perfect for us, isn't it?" This was a connection to her family that she cherished, and with the baby on the way, that felt especially important right now.

"It really is. Which is why I think we just buy the other two units on our floor and figure it out later. I'll move out of my place and we'll call an architect about connecting the units."

"Four units? Are you crazy?"

He waited for her to file first through the revolving doors. "No, I'm not crazy," he said when he'd joined her seconds later in the lobby. "It's a great investment, with no horrible neighbors to worry about, and it gives us flexibility to figure everything out." He pressed the button for the elevator. "Sound good?"

She didn't have a single complaint. Which wasn't like her when it came to Michael. So this was the new normal. "I'm sure Sawyer will be thrilled." The elevator dinged and the doors slid open. They stepped on board. "So, does this mean that our race is over?

I'm not really sure how we're supposed to figure out the winner."

Michael gathered her up in his arms and lifted her off her feet, placing the softest and sexiest kiss yet on her lips. Compared to their other kisses in the Grand Legacy elevator, this was the best one yet. "It doesn't matter. I already got the prize."

* * * * *

If you liked this story of pregnancy and passion, pick up these other novels from Karen Booth!

PREGNANT BY THE RIVAL CEO
THE BEST MAN'S BABY
THE TEN-DAY BABY TAKEOVER
PREGNANT BY THE BILLIONAIRE

Available now from Harlequin Desire!
***
And don't miss the next LITTLE SECRETS *story*
LITTLE SECRETS: HIS PREGNANT SECRETARY
by Joanne Rock
Available December 2017!

***

If you're on Twitter, tell us what you think of Harlequin Desire! #harlequindesire

*Can a former bad boy and the woman
he never forgot find true love during one
unforgettable Christmas?
Find out in CHRISTMASTIME COWBOY,
the sizzling new COPPER RIDGE novel from
New York Times bestselling author Maisey Yates.
Read on for your sneak peek...*

Liam Donnelly was nobody's favorite.

Though being a favorite in their household growing up would never have meant much, Liam was confident that as much as both of his parents disdained their younger son, Alex, they hated Liam more.

And as much as his brothers loved him—or whatever you wanted to call their brand of affection—Liam knew he wasn't the one they'd carry out if there was a house fire. That was fine, too.

It wasn't self-pity. It was just a fact.

But while he wasn't anyone's particular favorite, he knew he was at least one person's least favorite.

Sabrina Leighton hated him with every ounce of her beautiful, petite being. Not that he blamed her. But, considering they were having a business meeting today, he did hope that she could keep some of the hatred bottled up.

Liam got out of his truck and put his cowboy hat on, surveying his surroundings. The winery spread was beautiful, with a large, picturesque house overlooking the grounds. The winery and the road leading up to it were carved into an Oregon mountainside. Trees and forest surrounded the facility on three sides, creating a secluded feeling. Like the winery was part of another world. In front of the first renovated barn was a sprawling lawn and a path that led down to the river. There was a seating area there and Liam knew that during the warmer months it was a nice place to hang out. Right now, it was too damned cold, and the damp air that blew up from the rushing water sent a chill straight through him.

He shoved his hands in his pockets and kept on walking. There were three rustic barns on the property that they used for weddings and dinners, and one that had been fully remodeled into a dining and tasting room.

He had seen the new additions online. He hadn't actually been to Grassroots Winery in the past thirteen years. That was part of the deal. The deal that had been struck back when Jamison Leighton was still owner of the place.

Back when Liam had been nothing more than a good-for-nothing, low-class troublemaker with a couple of misdemeanors to his credit.

Times changed.

Liam might still be all those things at heart, but

he was also a successful businessman. And Jamison Leighton no longer owned Grassroots.

Some things, however, hadn't changed. The presence of Sabrina Leighton being one of them.

It had been thirteen years. But he couldn't pretend he thought everything was all right and forgiven. Not considering the way she had reacted when she had seen him at Ace's bar the past few months.

Small towns. Like everybody was at the same party and could only avoid each other for so long.

If it wasn't at the bar, they would most certainly end up at a four-way stop at the same time, or in the same aisle at the grocery store.

But today's meeting would not be accidental. Today's meeting was planned. He wondered if something would get thrown at him. It certainly wouldn't be the first time.

He walked across the gravel lot and into the dining room. It was empty, since the facility—a rustic barn with a wooden chandelier hanging in the center—had yet to open for the day. There was a bar with stools positioned at the front, and tables set up around the room. Back when he had worked here, there had been one basic tasting room, and nowhere for anyone to sit. Most of the wine had been sent out to retail stores for sale, rather than making the winery itself some kind of destination.

He wondered when all of that had changed. He imagined it had something to do with Lindy, the new owner and ex-wife of Jamison Leighton's son, Damien. As far as Liam knew, and he knew enough—considering he didn't get involved with business ventures without figuring out what he was getting into—Damien had drafted the world's dumbest prenuptial agreement. At least, it was dumb for a man who clearly had problems keeping his dick in his pants.

Though why Sabrina was still working at the winery when her sister-in-law had current ownership, and her brother had been deposed, and her parents were—from what he had read in public records—apoplectic about the loss of their family legacy, he didn't know. But he assumed he would find out. At about the same time he found out whether or not something was going to get thrown at his head.

The door from the back opened, and he gritted his teeth. Because, no matter how prepared he felt philosophically to see Sabrina, he knew that there would be impact. There always was. A damned funny thing, that one woman could live in the back of his mind the way she had for so long. That no matter how many years or how many women he put between them, she still burned bright and hot in his memory.

That no matter that he had steeled himself to run into her—because he knew how small towns worked—the impact was like a brick to the side of his head every single time.

She appeared a moment after the door opened,

looking severe. Overly so. Her blond hair was pulled back into a high ponytail, and she was wearing a black sheath dress that went down past her knees but conformed to curves that were more generous than they'd been thirteen years ago.

In a good way.

"Hello, Liam," she said, her tone impersonal. Had she not used his first name, it might have been easy to pretend that she didn't know who he was.

"Sabrina."

"Lindy told me that you wanted to talk about a potential joint venture. And since that falls under my jurisdiction as manager of the tasting room, she thought we might want to work together."

Now she was smiling.

The smile was so brittle it looked like it might crack her face.

"Yes, I'm familiar with the details. Particularly since this venture was my idea." He let a small silence hang there for a beat before continuing. "I'm looking at an empty building on the end of Main Street. It would be more than just a tasting room. It would be a small café with some retail space."

"How would it differ from Lane Donnelly's store? She already offers specialty foods."

"Well, we would focus on Grassroots wine and Laughing Irish cheese. Also, I would happily purchase products from Lane's to give the menu a local focus. The café would be nothing big. Just a small lunch place with wine. Very limited selection. Very specialty. But I feel like in a tourist location, that's what you want."

"Great," she said, her smile remaining completely immobile.

He took that moment to examine her more closely. The changes in her face over the years. She was more beautiful now than she had been at seventeen. Her slightly round, soft face had refined in the ensuing years, her cheekbones now more prominent, the angle of her chin sharper.

Her eyebrows looked different, too. When she'd been a teenager, they'd been thinner, rounder. Now they were a bit stronger, more angular.

"Great," he returned. "I guess we can go down and have a look at the space sometime this week. Gage West is the owner of the property, and he hasn't listed it yet. Handily, my sister-in-law is good friends with his wife. Both of my sisters-in-law, actually. So I got the inside track on that."

Her expression turned bland. "How impressive."

She sounded absolutely unimpressed. "It wasn't intended to be impressive. Just useful."

She sighed slowly. "Did you have a day of the week in mind to go view the property? Because I really am very busy."

"Are you?"

"Yes," she responded, that smile spreading over

her face again. "This is a very demanding job, plus I do have a life."

She stopped short of saying exactly what that life entailed.

"Too busy to do this, which is part of your actual job?" he asked.

On the surface she looked calm, but he could sense a dark energy beneath that spoke of a need to savage him. "I had my schedule sorted out for the next couple of weeks. This is coming together more quickly than expected."

"I'll work something out with Gage and give Lindy a call, how about that?"

"You don't have to call Lindy. I'll give you my phone number. You can call or text me directly."

She reached over to the counter and took a card from the rustic surface, extending her hand toward him. He reached out and took the card, their fingertips brushing as they made the handoff.

And he felt it. Straight down to his groin, where he had always felt things for her, even though it was impossible. Even though he was all wrong for her. And even though now they were doing a business deal together, and she looked like she would cheerfully chew through his flesh if given half the chance.

She might be smiling, but he didn't trust that smile. He was still waiting. Waiting for her to shout recriminations at him now that they were alone. Every other time he had encountered her over the past four months it had been in public. Twice in Ace's bar, and once walking down the street, where she had made a very quick sharp left to avoid walking past him.

It had not been subtle, and it had certainly not spoken of somebody who was over the past.

So his assumption had been that if the two of them were ever alone she was going to let him have it. But she didn't. Instead, she gave him that card and then began to look...bored.

"Did you need anything else?" she asked.

"Not really. Though I have some spreadsheet information that you might want to look over. Ideas that I have for the layout, the menu. It is getting a little ahead of ourselves, in case we end up not liking the venue."

"You've been to look at the venue already, haven't you?" It was vaguely accusatory.

"I have been there, yes. But again, I believe in preparedness. I was hardly going to get very deep into this if I didn't think it was viable. Personally, I'm interested in making sure that we have diverse interests. The economy doesn't typically favor farms, Sabrina. And that is essentially what my brothers and I have. I expect an uphill fight to make that place successful."

She tilted her head to the side. "Like you said, you do your research."

Her friendliness was beginning to slip. And he waited. For something else. For something to get thrown at him. It didn't happen.

"That I do. Take these," he said, handing her the folder that he was holding on to. He made sure their fingers didn't touch this time. "And we'll talk next week."

Then he turned and walked away from her, and he resisted the strong impulse to turn back and get one more glance at her. It wasn't the first time he had resisted that.

He had a feeling it wouldn't be the last.

As soon as Liam walked out of the tasting room, Sabrina let out a breath that had been killing her to keep in. A breath that contained about a thousand insults and recriminations. And more than a few very colorful swear word combinations. A breath that nearly burned her throat, because it was full of so many sharp and terrible things.

She lifted her hands to her face and realized they were shaking. It had been thirteen years. Why did he still affect her like this? Maybe, just maybe, if she had ever found a man who made her feel even half of what Liam did, she wouldn't have such a hard time dealing with him. The feelings wouldn't be so strong.

But she hadn't. So that supposition was basically moot.

The worst part was the tattoos. He'd had about three when he'd been nineteen. Now they covered both of his arms, and she had the strongest urge to make them as familiar to her as the original tattoos had been. To memorize each and every detail about them.

The tree was the one that really caught her attention. The Celtic knots, she knew, were likely a nod to his Irish heritage, but the tree—whose branches she could see stretching down from his shoulder— she was curious about what that meant.

"And you are spending too much time thinking about him," she admonished herself.

She shouldn't be thinking about him at all. She should just focus on congratulating herself for saying nothing stupid. At least she hadn't cried and demanded answers for the night he had completely laid waste to her every feeling.

"How did it go?"

Sabrina turned and saw her sister-in-law, Lindy, come in. People would be forgiven for thinking that she and Lindy were actually biological sisters. In fact, they looked much more alike than Sabrina and her younger sister Beatrix did.

Like Sabrina, Lindy had long, straight blond hair. Bea, on the other hand, had freckles all over her face and a wild riot of reddish-brown curls that resisted taming almost as strongly as the youngest Leighton sibling herself did.

That was another thing Sabrina and Lindy had in common. They were predominantly tame. At least, they kept things as together as they possibly could on the surface.

"Fine."

"You didn't savage him with a cheese knife?"

"Lindy," Sabrina said, "please. This is dry-clean only." She waved her hand up and down, indicating her dress.

"I don't know what your whole issue is with him…"

Because no one spoke of it. Lindy had married Sabrina's brother after the unpleasantness. It was no secret that Sabrina and her father were estranged—even if it was a brittle, quiet estrangement. But unless Damien had told Lindy the details—and Sabrina doubted he knew all of them—her sister-in-law wouldn't know the whole story.

"I don't have an issue with him," Sabrina said. "I knew him thirteen years ago. That has nothing to do with now. It has nothing to do with this new venture for the winery. Which I am on board with one hundred percent." It was true. She was.

"Well," Lindy said, "that's good to hear."

She could tell that Lindy didn't believe her. "It's going to be fine. I'm looking forward to this." That was also true. Mostly. She was looking forward to expanding Grassroots. Looking forward to helping build the winery and making it into something that was truly theirs. So that her parents could no longer shout recriminations about Lindy stealing something from the Leighton family.

Eventually, they would make the winery so much more successful that most of it would be theirs.

And if her own issues with her parents were tangled up in all of this, then…that was just how it was.

Sabrina wanted it all to work, and work well. If for no other reason than to prove to Liam Donnelly that she was no longer the seventeen-year-old girl whose world he'd wrecked all those years ago.

In some ways, Sabrina envied the tangible ways in which Lindy had been able to exact revenge on Damien. Of course, Sabrina's relationship with Liam wasn't anything like a ten-year marriage ended by infidelity. She gritted her teeth. She did her best not to think about Liam. About the past. Because it hurt. Every damn time it hurt. It didn't matter if it should or not.

But now that he was back in Copper Ridge, now that she sometimes just happened to run into him, it was worse. It was harder not to think about him.

Him and the grand disaster that had happened after.

* * * * *

*Look for CHRISTMASTIME COWBOY,
available from Maisey Yates and HQN Books
wherever books are sold.*

COMING NEXT MONTH FROM

HARLEQUIN *Desire*

Available December 5, 2017

YOU CAN FIND MORE INFORMATION ON UPCOMING HARLEQUIN® TITLES, FREE EXCERPTS AND MORE AT WWW.HARLEQUIN.COM.

HDCNM1117

SPECIAL EXCERPT FROM

HARLEQUIN®
Desire

*Bane Westmoreland's SEAL team is made up of
sexy alpha males.*

*Don't miss Laramie "Coop" Cooper's story
HIS SECRET SON
from* New York Times *bestselling author Brenda Jackson!*

*The SEAL who fathered Bristol's son died a hero's death...or
so she was told. But now Coop is back and vowing to claim
his child! Her son deserves to know his father, so Bristol must
find a way to fight temptation...and keep her heart safe.*

*Read on for a sneak peek at
HIS SECRET SON,
part of* **THE WESTMORELAND LEGACY** *series.*

Laramie stared at Bristol. "You were pregnant?"

"Yes," she said in a soft voice. "And you're free to order a
paternity test if you need to verify that my son is yours."

He had a son? It took less than a second for his emotions to
go from shock to disbelief. "How?"

She lifted a brow. "Probably from making love almost
nonstop for three solid days."

They had definitely done that. Although he'd used a condom
each and every time, he knew there was always a possibility
that something could go wrong.

"And where is he?" he asked.

"At home."

Where the hell was that? It bothered him how little he knew about the woman who'd just announced she'd given birth to his child. At least she'd tried contacting him to let him know. Some women would not have done so.

If his child had been born nine months after their holiday fling, that meant he would have turned two in September. While Laramie was in a cell, somewhere in the world, Bristol had been giving life.

To his child.

Emotions Laramie had never felt before suddenly bombarded him with the impact of a Tomahawk missile. He was a parent, which meant he had to think about someone other than himself. He wasn't sure how he felt about that. But then, wasn't he used to taking care of others as a member of his SEAL team?

She nodded. "I'm not asking you for anything Laramie, if that's what you're thinking. I just felt you had a right to know about the baby."

She wasn't asking him for anything? Did she not know her bold declaration that he'd fathered her child demanded everything?

"I want to see him."

"You will. I would never keep Laramie from you."

"You named him Laramie?" Even more emotions swamped him. Her son—their son—had his name?

She hesitated. "Yes."

Then he asked. "So, what's your reason for giving yourself my last name, as well?"

Don't miss
HIS SECRET SON
by New York Times *bestselling author Brenda Jackson,*
available December 2017
wherever Harlequin® Desire books and ebooks are sold.

www.Harlequin.com

HDEXP1117